She Found Me

Joy Mullett

J M Publications Limited

Copyright © 2024 Joy Mullett

All rights reserved

The characters and events portrayed in this book are fictitious. Any similarity to real persons, living or dead, is coincidental and not intended by the author.

No part of this book may be reproduced, or stored in a retrieval system, or transmitted in any form or by any means, electronic, mechanical, photocopying, recording, or otherwise, without express written permission of the publisher.

*To my family and friends who have always believed in me.
To you, the reader, thank you for giving my work a chance.
To the universe, for making my dreams come true.*

Contents

Title Page
Copyright
Dedication
Authors Note
Books in this series:
She Found Me

Prologue	1
Chapter 1	2
Chapter 2	12
Chapter 3	25
Chapter 4	32
Chapter 5	43
Chapter 6	55
Chapter 7	61
Chapter 8	67
Chapter 9	75

Chapter 10	79
Chapter 11	89
Chapter 12	97
Chapter 13	104
Chapter 14	112
Chapter 15	117
Chapter 16	126
Chapter 17	139
Chapter 18	147
Chapter 19	155
Chapter 20	166
Chapter 21	174
Chapter 22	183
Chapter 23	187
Chapter 24	191
Acknowledgement	203
About The Author	205

Authors Note

Please be aware this book is intended for mature audiences ages 18 and over.

The story includes open door romance, along with some darker themes, including kidnapping, violence and murder.

However, the main focus is on the relationship of a power couple.

If you are okay with this, please continue and enjoy!

Joy x

Books in this series:

I've Found Her- Bella and Damien
I've Found Her part 2 - Chloe and Josh
He Found Me - Katie and Leo
She Found Me - Marco and Mia

With more to come from Katie and Leo later in the year.

All books are available on Amazon.

Follow Joy on social media @jemullettbooks for her latest releases and updates.

She Found Me

By Joy Mullett

Prologue

Marco

Italy is a country of passion and beauty, art, and history. It is also a country of corruption and division. Italy has a notorious underworld—an underworld that I, Marco Guerra rule.

Being the leader of an organisation like the Guerra has its challenges. Mentally and physically. Execution and torture, some would say, are among those challenges. But for me those types of tasks are the most fulfilling, as they are the times when I release my anger and frustration. It's the only time my brain and muscles relax.

No, my challenges are women. One woman in particular. I do not understand the female species. Why a man would want a woman around permanently is beyond me. Women, I require for one purpose only, and it is not necessary for them to even speak. I decide when I need a woman, not them.

Chapter 1

Marco

"What are you doing here?" I grumble at my uninvited visitor.

"It's Thursday," Mia announces sarcastically.

"I'm aware of what day it is. I asked what you are doing here."

"Come on, Marco. Today's our day." She walks further into my office as if she belongs here.

"What makes you think we have a *day*?"

"I came last Thursday and the Thursday before."

"Because I summoned you here. I have not contacted you today."

"Well, I'm here now." Mia puts her bag down and starts to unbutton her blouse.

Annoyed at her blatant disrespect, I stand forcefully from my desk. My chair slides from beneath me, banging into the wall at my back.

"Get out!" I boom.

Mia jumps, startled. "Marco, you know you want—"

"No, Mia. Do as I say when I say it and not before!"

Mia's nostrils flare. She grabs her bag and storms out of my office. As she does, her perfume makes its way across the room and soaks into my senses. I can smell her. I can taste her need. My cock stirs in anticipation. Growling at the protests of my body, I go after her.

"Stop!" I command.

She turns to face me at the front door. I use my body to push her against it. Both my hands wrap around her neck. I feel her heart rate quicken. She tips her head back. Her mouth opens slightly.

"Why do you continue to disrespect me? Disobedience does not go unpunished, Mia. Get back in there and beg for my forgiveness."

One side of her mouth curls up into a smirk, an eyebrow rises, and her eyes twinkle beneath her lashes. Oh, Mia is a bad girl.

After teaching Mia a lesson neither of us will forget for a while, it is back to business.

The Guerra have always had a very close relationship with the head of police. This year has seen changes that I am not happy with, including the replacement of that chief, thus breaking our close relationship. It is time I paid our new chief a little visit.

Van has the car ready when I leave the house. Once I'm settled in the back, he gives me a nod through the rear-view mirror and pulls out of the driveway. Another car, containing my men, follows closely behind us. The weather is surprisingly dull today, considering the time of year. Dark clouds are approaching up ahead. I don't like rain. But today the inevitable storm does nothing to dampen my mood. Today I am in an unusually good mood. It must be Chief Lorenzo's lucky day.

As we walk through the police station, my men stay one pace behind me, their steps in time with my own. A couple of officers try and prevent our intrusion, but I don't stop when they stand in my path, and inevitably their inferior bodies bounce off mine, which knocks them to the floor. We walk into Lorenzo's office, but he doesn't seem surprised by my invasion.

"Guerra, to what do I owe the pleasure?" Lorenzo's sarcastic tone has my blood boiling.

"It has come to my attention that many of my workers have been arrested."

"Oh, and have they committed a crime?" Lorenzo asks, playing dumb.

"They have been arrested during our allocated windows," I explain firmly.

"I don't understand what you mean by allocated windows." Lorenzo sits back in his chair, trying to look unaffected by me.

I bang my fists on his desk, sending papers flying on to the floor.

"Don't fuck with me, Lorenzo. The Guerras have had this arrangement for generations. You are playing with fire if you think you have any influence in changing that."

"Oh, I'm not fucking with you, Marco Guerra. I'm deadly serious. You are not the law. I am. And things are going to change around here."

"Over my dead body!" I fire back.

Lorenzo smirks. "Be careful what you wish for, Mr. Guerra."

I leave before I put a bullet between his eyes, but not before throwing his desk over and smashing his lamp.

Lorenzo doesn't react, but his face has an expression I can't read.

Mia

After leaving Marco's house feeling satisfied, I get into my convertible, put on my sunglasses, touch up my glossy red lips, and set off down the driveway. I don't need to look into the rear-view mirror to know that Marco is watching me leave.

He may be the boss of the Guerra empire, but he is not the boss of me. Marco thinks he is in control of our arrangement. Although we are nothing serious, he is far from in control. I have him just where I want him.

Vista Mare is a beautiful restaurant overlooking the sea, hence the name. This is where I am meeting my friends for lunch. I pull up at the front, where my door is opened, and a hand appears to help me out of my car. The restaurant doesn't have valet parking, but nothing is too much trouble for them where I am concerned. I hand the handsome gentleman my keys, and he gives me wink. Walking into the restaurant, I feel his eyes roaming up and down my red dress. He's not the only one. I'm not oblivious to the heads that turn when I walk into a room. The women want to be me, and the men want to be in me. Confidently I strut through the restaurant with a big smile and my head held high. The restaurant manager leads me to my usual table, where I find my girls waiting for me.

"Mia!" The three of them stand and each give me an overexaggerated hug and kiss, as if they didn't see me just yesterday. Out of the three of them, I trust Emmaline the most. We haven't even known each other that long, but I know I could tell her anything and it wouldn't go any further. Unlike the other two on the opposite side of the table. I've known these girls since school. They've followed me around like two lost sheep since they realised who I was. I couldn't have gotten rid of them if I'd wanted to. Being friends with Mia Alboni gives you status, and it's the status they want. To be honest, I have used them just as much as they have used me. They're both attractive girls, so as a group, we attract attention, and I use this to my advantage. They're a good distraction when I need to escape from somewhere or a next-best thing if I can't be bothered attending an event.

The girls order champagne, as of course they know I will cover the bill. They'll do their "Oh no, Mia, you paid last time—I'll get this" routine as always, knowing full well it would empty their bank accounts if they did. I know exactly how much they get paid because I pay their wages. I also know how extravagant their lifestyles are and that they literally live from payday to payday. They don't earn a great deal, but on the other hand, they don't do a great deal either. Both Lucia and Marisa are influencers for my makeup brand. Each of them is your stereotypical good-looking girl who has, let's say, "enhanced" herself with fillers, and fakeness. They often get asked if they're twins, which they are not. But they look good on film, and I'm more than happy for them to be the faces of my social media. It's what sells, and it means I don't have to get involved.

"Are there any allergies we need to be aware of? I know of Miss Alboni's nut allergy, but are there any others?" the waiter asks as he pours the champagne while we scan the menu.

"Not for me, thank you." Emmaline covers her glass. "I'm driving. I've got to pick Alfie up from school later."

Emmaline is so beautiful inside and out. She sits beside me in a white cotton sundress, fresh faced, her hair in loose waves, and is certainly the most attractive woman in the restaurant. I envy her. To be able to just be herself. To leave her house in whatever she feels comfortable in and not have to worry about what people think of her.

"Right, girls," I say, addressing Lucia and Marisa. "We have the brand launch event in London coming up. Make sure you read the information I have emailed to you. You don't need to do anything—I have arranged it all. Just ensure you know the new products inside out. Oh, and go over the guest list to make sure I haven't missed off anyone of high influence." I then turn to Emmaline. "Are you sure you won't come?"

Emmaline declines. "Thank you, but no. I can't leave my son. Plus, I'll stay and make sure everything is okay while you're gone."

After lunch, we say goodbye to Emmaline, who generously tips the staff, as I wouldn't let her pay for her meal. Lucia and Marisa jump in the back of my open-top car, sitting on the backs of the seats rather than where their bums are supposed be. Annoyed at the disrespect for my leather seats, I put my foot down as I set off, throwing them back just enough that the bottle of champagne they brought with them from the restaurant spills in their faces as they pass it between them, drinking from the bottle. Honestly, anyone would think they're in their early twenties, not thirties.

Driving through the town, I have my music on loud to cover their annoying giggles and chatter while they take selfies. As soon as the car is parked, I grab my Bottega Veneta handbag and make my way up the cream-coloured stone street. The girls hurry after me, their heels clip-clapping on the stones as they rush to catch up with me.

This street is my favourite shopping destination, home to a wealth of world-renowned fashion houses, designer boutiques, and high-end department stores. I make sure I'm seen here at least once a week. The need to keep up appearances means I frequent here much more often than I would choose, but at least it's a beautiful place to be. I'm in awe every time I visit, taking in the stunning architecture and historic buildings. Plus, I do like a nice handbag, so I put up with it.

Being part of the Guerra organisation brings great responsibilities. Although my family isn't part of the main bloodline, the men in my family have always played very important roles. My father is a retired consigliere, the right-hand man, advisor, and trusted friend of one of the late Guerra leaders. My brother now takes on this role for Marco Guerra, the current man in charge. Marco. The thought of him makes my heart beat a little faster. The excitement and thrill I got from being around him this morning makes me smile.

Our first shop is MIA. MIA is my worldwide cosmetics brand. The stores are exclusive to Italy, but I have a revised range in all good beauty retailers across the world. It's all excitement when we arrive. We have a maximum number policy so that customers can have a more relaxed shopping experience. We found that during Covid, we made more money with the restrictions. As people had spent time queuing to get in the store, when they actually got inside, they made the most of their time in there. Instead of running in and just getting what they needed, they browsed almost every item. On average people spend double the amount per visit than before our restrictions.

I make a fuss of all our lovely customers queuing outside. I take selfies with them, chat about their favourite products, and thank them for coming. Inside, the girls and I pose for images to use on our social media and marketing campaigns. The MIA brand is exclusively black, red, and glitter, from the packaging to the products. If it's not sparkly, it's not MIA. The funny thing is, I don't use any of the MIA range. I don't do glitter, and our fragranced products are far too sweet for me.

Moving on, we browse the boutiques and

department stores, buying a range of accessories for me and the girls. As usual it's my black credit card that takes the hit.

After speaking to the locals and enforcing the Guerras omnipresence, I leave Lucia and Marisa and head home.

Home is my happy place. This is where I feel like myself. My home is in a rural part of Italy. Set back from the main road, the house is an old farmhouse and barn I converted. A lot of the work I did myself, knocking walls down, painting, and even tiling. I may have immaculate nails, but I don't mind getting my hands dirty. I'm far from a princess.

Chapter 2

Mia

The first thing I do when I get in is head to the bathroom. I tie up my hair, strip out of my tight red dress, and get into the shower. I wash off my makeup along with my day, leaving Mia the brand behind until tomorrow. Because that's all I am when I'm out there. I have a job to do, and I take my role in the Guerra seriously. But that's my job, and now it's me time. Once I'm makeup free and refreshed, I put on my comfy shorts, vest top, and trainers and head out.

The smell as I go outside has me smiling. The back of my house is surrounded by fruit trees. Trees I planted when I moved here. The Guerras are known for their lemons, but I prefer apples and oranges. I pull an apple from the tree and bring it to my lips, and I inhale before taking a bite. So delicious and juicy. After pottering around my garden for ten minutes, I mount my quad bike, which is parked at the side of the house. I quickly start the engine and ride through the acres of land to my sanctuary.

As I pull up, Alfie, Emmaline's son, comes out to meet me. He waves, excitedly beckoning me to get in quickly.

"It's time, Mia. Come quick. Rosie's having her babies."

Sure enough, when I enter, I find Emmaline comforting our latest rescue, a spaniel cross who is in full labour.

"Wow, Rosie, you're doing so well. You're such a good girl." I give her head a stroke and scratch behind her ears.

"Hey, you're distracting her," Emmaline jokes, batting me away. Emmaline just wants the best view. She has been caring for Rosie for the past week, making sure everything was ready for the new arrivals. By the looks of the labouring mother, the puppies should arrive very soon. It's only fair that Emmaline gets to see all the best bits.

Soon enough, the puppies arrive one by one. Emmaline checks them over and hands them to the new mum to clean and feed. Alfie and I watch in awe, the miracle of life happening before us. We now have five new animals to take care of in the sanctuary, however these little beauties will be adopted once they're old enough. That takes our current total to 105.

I opened the sanctuary about twelve months ago when my house got too crowded with the dogs and cats I had taken in. Most of the animals

I rescue are strays. The poor things had been abandoned or were perhaps born on the streets due to their parents being previously rejected and dumped, many of them with medical conditions. Most of the animals won't ever leave the sanctuary. People don't want to adopt an animal with extra needs and additional expenses or an older animal that only has a few years left. This was my reason for taking all these animals in. I want every animal to live all their days, especially their last days, in a comfortable, loving environment. That is what I have created here in the sanctuary.

I designed the building myself, as a home from home. There are no cages or crates. We have a living room with sofas and chairs, bean bags, and rugs. There's a fireplace and a television. All the windows are to the floor so the animals can sit and look outside. The dogs especially enjoy barking at the postman when he arrives—oh, and the window cleaners get a good barking at too.

Then we have the playroom, where the dogs and cats play with toys and run and climb on the soft play equipment. The kitchen has separate areas where the animals can eat individually or as a group. Some of the animals, when they arrive, aren't used to being in such close proximity with other animals, especially another species of animal. It doesn't usually take long for them to settle in, though. The eating situation, however, can be a bit difficult. We cater for all their needs, even the grumpy ones who don't like to share.

The bathroom has walk-in showers and a big, raised bath. In the bedroom, we make sure there is a suitable bed or basket for each animal. They're each given a new one with their name on it when they arrive. Funnily enough, most of the animals stick to their own beds. We also have extras in there and large cushions in foam kennels in case any of them want to snuggle up, which many do. We dim the light in here during the day. We do this so that the older ones always have a place to go that is calm and relaxed. Each room has a dog and cat flap that take them outside to the *business* area. These areas are restricted and were designed purely for them to do their *business*.

Outside, we have acres and acres of grass and woodland that the animals get to explore every day. The sanctuary is also starting to expand with other animals now. It wasn't planned, but how could I say no to a three-legged rabbit and a blind guinea pig? That's the next project. A barn building of some description, as it looks like we will also be taking on chickens and a pair of billy goats.

I fund the sanctuary myself, but I have a long list of volunteers who love and care for the animals. We do a lot of pet therapy sessions. Some we run here, where people will come and look after them for day, go for a walk with them, or just sit and watch television with them. Then we have days where we take some of our more relaxed animals out into the community, nursing homes, hospitals and so on, like a therapy treatment. I do have my paid staff who do these activities and run the sanctuary twenty-four-seven. Although I pay the expenses, we do charge for some things, like the sale of puppies and the training and experience days we run. Even though the sanctuary is a charity, we cannot have civilians thinking the Guerra are soft. No, the only reason I am allowed to own such an organisation as this is that—how did my father put it again? Ahh yes, it "enforces once again that the Guerra are in charge of everything, even charity."

Emmaline is one of my volunteers. She and Alfie come up here twice a week. Alfie adores the animals. He wants to be a vet when he's older. Emmaline refuses to take any payment for her time, as she says she does it because she enjoys it, and it's something she and Alfie can do together. So instead, I give the money to Alfie. I'm not sure about Emmaline's money situation. They live a modest life in a nice three-bed cottage, but Emmaline doesn't work, and my instinct tells me she isn't very wealthy.

Once all the puppies have been checked and have their coloured ribbon collars so we can tell them apart, Emmaline and Alfie settle them in a quiet area of the bedroom. Alfie kisses each one good night, promising to see them tomorrow.

"Thank you so much for your help today, Alfie. Here are your wages." I hand Alfie an envelope.

"Thanks, Mia. You know I'm saving up for my own sanctuary just like this. And then, when I'm a vet, I am going to make all the sick animals better."

"I know you will, Alfie. You will be a very good vet too."

Alfie beams, and the two of them leave along with their dog Macy, who always comes with them for a play with the other animals.

The rest of the evening passes quickly. There's always something that needs doing. A puddle made by one of the older ones who didn't make it outside or a laundry wash that needs going on. Once we are straight, I settle down in the living area on one of the bean bags. As soon as my bum touches down, I'm swarmed with furballs. Everyone wants cuddles and scratches behind their ears. This is my favourite part of the day.

I'm just dozing off when my phone rings. It's my brother Van.

"Mia?!" There's no pleasantries from my brother. Straight to the point.

"Van, how are you?"

"There's an event tomorrow I need you to attend. Lorenzo's throwing himself a coronation party." Van continues, ignoring my question.

"A what? Is that a thing when someone becomes the Chief of Police?" I ask.

"No. It's a coverup for something. I need you go and find out who is there. See what you can find out."

"Yes, no problem. Where and when?"

"Villa Mico. The car will pick you up at 7:30 p.m." And the line goes dead.

"Yeah, see ya, brother," I mumble to myself. Well, I better get to bed. Looks like I have a late night ahead of me tomorrow.

Before I go to sleep, I text Lucia and Marisa, who respond immediately. They are always up for a free glam night out. Both of them are good at influencing the opposite sex—and the same sex for that matter. I have no doubt the three of us will get what Van needs.

The girls arrive just after noon. They immediately raid my walk-in wardrobe for their outfits and accessories.

"Oh wow, Mia, when did you get this?" Lucia walks back into my bedroom holding a red silk dress against herself.

"That one arrived last week. There's another box in the corner with more from the same designer."

Marisa's ears prick up, and she instantly goes in search of said box.

"You can wear anything you want, bar that one, Lucia," I tell her.

"Of course. Red is your colour." Lucia blows me a kiss.

Red is my signature colour. It may be my full outfit, my accessories, or just my lips, but you will always see Mia Alboni wearing red, the colour of blood.

Marisa undresses before trying on a number of the samples.

"I wish people would send me free stuff. You're so lucky, Mia."

I definitely would not call myself lucky. Sure, being who I am, in the family I was born into, does have its perks. But it also comes with a whole lot of shit.

Not breaking my character, even in front of my friends, I reply sternly, "Nothing is *free,* Marisa." Standing up from my bed where I have been watching them, I glare at her. "If they want the protection of the Guerra, they must pay for it."

"Of course. I didn't mean…."

"Whatever. I have something to take care of before I get ready. The makeup and hair stylists will be here any minute. You two go first."

I leave the room, slamming the door slightly as I leave. I'm not in the mood for their materialistic nonsense right now. Unfortunately, we lost one of our dogs last night. He was an old boy and had lived his best life since he was brought here twelve months ago. But Barney the Second meant a lot to me. He was the first dog I rescued when I opened the sanctuary. He had reminded me of the first dog I ever rescued off the street.

When I was twelve, a dog followed me home from school. He had a limp in his front paw. He was obviously a street dog and had wanted help. When I got home, I took him into our shed and looked at his paw. He was so gentle and let me clean the wound he had in his pad. I found a small piece of glass, which I removed. Once I cleaned it and put a bandage around it, he gave me so may kisses as if he was thanking me. For weeks, I looked after him, feeding him and playing with him after school, until one day I came home and found him with a bullet in his head. My dad had found him. I broke down in tears, cradling his limp blood-covered body.

"You will learn from this, Mia," my father boomed from behind me. "You are an Alboni. Part of the Guerra. Never get attached to anything or anyone. Attachment makes you weak." He then threw me a spade.

"Get rid of it," he spat.

Growing up, I knew my dad was a bad man. But that was the first time I realised how cruel he could be. And it only got worse after that.

I carried horrendous guilt with me from then on. If only I had let Barney the First go after I had healed his paw, he would have lived. So, when I saw Barney the Second on the same street all those years later, I knew what I had to do. If my dad dares to come near any of my animals now, I will put a bullet in his head before I let them be harmed, and he knows it. I'm not a soft little girl anymore.

When I arrive at the sanctuary, I find Emmaline and Alfie at the memorial area. Barney the Second isn't the first animal we have lost, and he won't be the last. But it doesn't get any easier for any of us. All the staff gather round as his ashes are scattered. A perk of being part of the Guerra is that I get to use the company furnace. Alfie reads a poem, and we all take a minute to reflect on our fur friend's cheekiness.

"Be careful tonight, Mia," Emmaline warns as we make our way back to my house.

I don't involve Emmaline in of the Guerra business, but I do tell her what my plans are.

"Don't worry about me. Just a regular night for Mia Alboni." I gently squeeze her hand that she has looped through my arm.

We discuss plans for the sanctuary over a coffee in my kitchen. I had almost forgotten about my evening out until the girls shouted to hurry me up. After seeing Emmaline and Alfie out, I head up to my dressing room. Lucia and Marisa's voices are high-pitched and louder than usual, meaning they are already drunk. Great. The dressing room is a mess—clothes and accessories all over the floor, champagne glasses everywhere, and what looks like fake tan spilt over my white carpet. Closing my eyes, I take a deep breath.

"Mia, come on. Where have you been?" Marisa beckons me over.

"We've started without you. You'll have to catch up. Here." Lucia pours, then hands me a glass of whatever they're drinking.

After a quick shower, I sit at my dressing table to get my hair and makeup done. Van has sent me some photos of men to look out for and instructions on what to do. I do a little research on these men myself. Van never tells me exactly what is going on, but I usually find out my own way.

The limo arrives at 7:30 on the dot, and we also have an SUV of men that follow behind us. Not that I need protection. I could take any of those men down in two seconds flat. On the way, I give the girls their instructions.

"We need as much information as possible. Their names, where they are from, and why they are there." The girls nod in unison. "That means everyone attending the party—men, women, old, young—not just the attractive men, Marisa, okay?"

"Got it," Marisa confirms.

We touch up our lipstick and respray our perfume before leaving the limo. With our heads head high and our shoulders back, in our unison walk the girls and I have down to a tee, we strut up the red carpet to the entrance. I notice the two doormen frantically looking through the papers on their clipboard and then back at me. I take my time walking up to them, maintaining eye contact with them. I can see sweat beginning to form on their brows.

"Gentlemen," I say, greeting them with a smile.

They both go pale in the face.

"Miss Alboni. Tonight's event is invitation only," one man stutters.

"I know," I reply sternly.

The man franticly searches through his list of names again. "I'm sorry, but I don't see your name on the invitation list."

"That's because I wasn't invited," I reply, irritated.

The men then look at each other again, clearly deciding which they would like to save, their jobs or their lives. It doesn't take them long to unlock the red rope stopping our entrance and wave us through. We are greeted by waiters with trays of champagne flutes and canapés. The girls take a drink each, along with a handful of food. I don't eat at events like this, when having a nut allergy, you can never be too careful.

"Okay, let's split up. We will meet in the ladies' room in one hour."

Scanning the room, I find the bar and make my way over. On the way, I am stopped by Chief Lorenzo himself.

Chapter 3

Mia

"Mia, what a pleasant surprise." He embraces me with a kiss on each cheek. "You look absolutely stunning." Lorenzo takes my hand and kisses my knuckles too. He then steps back to enjoy the view.

Tonight, I decided on a black silk dress with a red bag and red shoes, not forgetting my red lips. I see his wife watching us over his shoulder, so I give him a little twirl and accidently on purpose fall into him a little. Catching me by the waist, he clearly more than appreciates this. Out of the corner of my eye, I see Lorenzo's wife making her way towards us.

I stroke his arm while he speaks, which prompts him to lean in and whisper in my ear, "Why don't you join me in my private room for a welcome drink?" He moves the hair off my shoulder and runs the tips of his fingers down my arm.

My body wants to shiver in disgust, but I

hold it in. "I don't think your wife would approve of that, Chief Lorenzo. Do you?" I say a lot more loudly than needed.

"Approve of what?" snaps Lorenzo's wife.

Lorenzo moves away from me, scowling, before turning to his wife. "Oh, we were just having a little joke." Lorenzo puts his arm around his wife and turns her away from me. "Come on now, let me introduce you to someone who has been dying to meet you." They mingle within the crowd, soon disappearing from my view.

The bar is quite busy, but I find an opening between two very large men who have their backs to each other. Sitting on a bar stool causes my dress to open at the split, displaying my tanned, smooth legs. After ordering a margarita with salt, I sit and wait for the men beside me to notice. It doesn't take them long.

The first guy is Russian, and the other is Spanish. I can speak many different languages and I am very good at pronunciation and accent. When I go to England, people think I have lived there all my life, my English is so good, and it's the same with Spanish. Putting on my best British accent so as not to arouse suspicion, I soon have both men eating out of the palm of my hand. Each of the men are representatives of underground organisations. I recognise tattoos they have on their hands. Neither man is at the top of their hierarchy, but both must hold valuable and influential positions. As far as they know, both organisations have just been invited to celebrate Lorenzo's new position as chief. Both admit to having found the invitation strange, but they decided to attend out of curiosity.

What is that sneaky chief up to?

After humouring the guys for a while, I make my excuses and find Marisa and Lucia. It seems Lorenzo has invited members of each of the organised crime groups from Italy's surrounding countries. All countries have organised crime groups. Italy's main organisation is the Guerra, but the country also has our archenemy the Martelé, however there doesn't seem to be anyone from the Martelé here. Albeit Illegal, underground organisations are needed to keep the countries from going into chaos, so they generally work alongside the police. I cannot speak for all, but the Guerra have good values, protect their own, and have respect for civilians. We also respect our fellow countries' organisations and expect them to do the same. Their unannounced arrival at this event is not going to go down well with Marco.

Van doesn't say much when I ring and explain our findings. He never tells me anything. I'd love to know more and be part of all the excitement, but I am a female, so that means it is not my place. It's a protection thing, apparently, not a sexist thing. I've tried, believe me. I will just have to do what I normally do: find things out for myself. But it looks to me like Lorenzo is trying to make allies.

I buy us girls some drinks and let them go and enjoy the attention. All eyes are on them as they walk through the groups of people. Every man has a look, whether it is a blatant open-mouthed stare up and down or a sly peek over their glass so their partner doesn't notice. Marisa and Lucia own the room, and they love every second of it. They better make the most of it, as this party will be coming to an extremely abrupt end very soon.

Perched on a stool at the bar, I think over the event tonight. Surely Lorenzo would know that the Guerra would find out about his party and who was on the guest list. He would also know that the Guerra would not be happy. He wanted to piss Marco off. He also knows that Marco will not let this go. I have no doubt Marco will have also worked this out. It's quite clever when you think about it, really. Tonight the Guerra could storm in here and potentially start a war with every one of its surrounding countries. These people are all on our territory at the same time, and the Guerra must stand their ground.

I'm so deep in thought, I hadn't noticed the tall man appear beside me. I sense him looking my way, so I look at his face. A smile fills his strong jawline right up to his cheek bones. He's obviously amused by how deep in thought I was. Maybe he has spoken to me and I didn't realise.

"I'm sorry. I was in a world of my own."

His smile fades slightly as he looks into my eyes. His are deep and warming. Butterflies in my stomach have me breaking our connection.

"Would you like another drink?" He points at my half-full glass of champagne that has bright red lipstick on the rim.

"No, thank you. I will be leaving soon."

"That's a shame. It's Mia, isn't it?" He offers his hand to introduce himself. "I'm Ross."

When I place my hand in his, he doesn't shake it but turns it over, lightly rubbing my fingers with his thumb. I suddenly remember him. We have met before. He works for the police department.

"We've met before. Detective Rossini, isn't it?"

His eyebrows rise, and he smiles that smile again. "I wasn't sure if you would remember. Yes, we have met. A couple of times, actually."

I hadn't noticed before, but Detective Rossini is a very handsome man. He looks to be more suited to the Guerra rather than the police force, though. His large frame would fit in perfectly. His smile, on the other hand—maybe not.

"May I?" He points at the stool beside me.

"Of course."

As he sits down, his suit trousers strain over his thigh muscles and his aftershave fills my senses—delicious. I could definitely see myself sitting on his lap. Conversation comes really easy with him. He has me laughing and relaxing into the moment, forgetting where I am and why I am here. Suddenly my bubble bursts, and my walls are back up in full force. It's funny how I know when he is near. I don't need to turn around to know that Marco's eyes are burning into the back of my head from the doorway.

"I'm sorry, Ross, I really need to get going."

He looks genuinely disappointed. As I stand up off the stool, he stands, too, taking my hand and leaning into me.

"You are incredibly beautiful, Mia. I'd love to get to know you better. Could I have your number? I'd like to see you again, if you would like that, too, of course?"

I smile. I *would* like that, too, actually.

"Here's my card." I hand him my business card, kiss him on the cheek, then go and find my girls.

Once I have rounded them up, we make our way to the door. We are greeted by Marco with a face like thunder.

"Mia, a word." He storms out of the building and around the corner. The Guerra men are arriving and being briefed by Van. I leave Marisa and Lucia to swoon over my brother and follow Marco. What is his problem tonight?

Chapter 4

Mia

"What the hell are you playing at?" Marco booms at me once we are alone.

"Hey, don't you shout at me. If you have a problem, Marco, just say it."

"You throwing yourself at one of Lorenzo's men."

"I was not throwing myself at him. We were having a very nice conversation."

"What about?" Marco holds his fist tight at his side.

"Nothing that concerns you," I reply, irritated.

"Everything concerns me. And what did you give him?" he growls, clearly trying not to raise his voice.

"My business card," I reply, standing my ground. Most people would be afraid of Marco right now. But not me. I have grown up with men like Marco all my life.

"Why?"

"Because he wants to buy some new makeup. For fuck's sake, Marco, why do you think?" I am done with this conversation, so I push past him to go back inside. Before I take my third step, I am turned around by my arm.

Marco is holding my elbow tightly. "I forbid you see that man again." His eyes are open wider than I have ever seen them. He stares them into mine intently.

"Why, Marco? Why do you forbid me?" I demand, still holding his gaze.

He looks back and forth between my eyes. It takes what feels like minutes for him to reply. Dropping his eyes and loosening his grip on my elbow, he finally answers. "Because Guerras must never be associated with the police."

For a minute there, I thought he was going to say something else.

Marco and I have a sort of friends-with-benefits type of arrangement—only without the friendship. As human beings, we both have needs, and neither of us desires to be in any sort of relationship. I do not need or want a man in my life. From observing my mother and father's marriage, I've seen firsthand how controlling men can be. There has never been any love there. Just control. It happens to everyone. Even in the most loving relationships. Strong women with brilliant careers giving it all up for their husbands. They'll believe they wanted to give it all up for their children, to go part time and look after their home, but really, it is what is expected of them.

Some women manage to continue with their careers but will still be at home every evening while their other half goes out and enjoys themselves. Women get too tired to be able to put themselves first. A woman would ask their husband if they could go to an event. A man would simply tell a woman that they had an engagement —that's if they would even tell them at all. There is never any equality.

No, that life is not for me. I wouldn't even have this sort of relationship with Marco if I didn't have certain desires. But unfortunately, only men can fulfil those. And boy does Marco fill me— I mean *them*, the desires. It's perfect, really, as we have no worries about what each other thinks about us or what either of us do in our day-to-day lives. We live out our wildest, dirtiest fantasies without being embarrassed and then separate, feeling satisfied without another thought for each other. Or so I thought. Recently Marco has been acting strangely around me. Like tonight for example. If I didn't know better, I would say he was jealous. Yet the other Thursday when I went to his house, he almost threw me out. All this hot and cold behaviour is starting to piss me off. Maybe this arrangement has run its course. Shame. But there are more fish in the sea, so to speak. Like Detective Rossini for example.

I don't reply to Marco. I just sharply remove my arm from his grip and head back inside where I find the girls. Both of them look at me with questionable expressions after seeing Marco follow in behind me. They both know the situation.

"You know, I think Marco might be falling in love with you, Mia," Lucia whispers to me.

"Don't be ridiculous," I snap. The man has a heart of stone. They don't know him like I do. Marco just hates that he can't control me like he does everyone else in his life.

"Ladies, the car is waiting for you," Van informs us.

The girls totter over to the waiting limo, climbing straight in and closing the door. They know what's coming and are more than happy to be leaving before it starts. I stay in the entrance, waving them off.

"It's time to go." Marco growls from behind me.

"What, and miss all the fun? I don't think so." I spin on my heels and walk around him, returning to the main hall where the evening is in full swing.

After taking a drink from a passing waiter, I

find a quiet corner to observe, privately. From here, I can see all four entrances to the room. Each door opens in unison, and in walk the Guerra.

I take a deep breath as my heart skips a beat. My excitement builds as the sharply dressed men make their way around the edge of the room, surrounding all the guests. They don't notice at first, but when they do, the atmosphere soon changes. This is what I love. The power, the respect. Smiling behind my glass, I watch Marco make his way over to the stage. The band stops playing as he reaches them. As he takes one of the microphones from its stand, the room falls silent, all eyes on him. Marco is so masculine, he looks nonhuman. He's a beast of a man. He towers above everyone. His shoulders are so wide, he only just fits through an open door. His voice is so deep, you feel the vibrations. Each muscle in his body is prominently shaped beneath his skin. Dark hair covers his body. Thinking about him makes my core fill with heat. I just want him to pick me up, throw me over his shoulder, and take me to bed.

"Good evening, ladies and gentlemen, Lorenzo." Marco spits Lorenzo's name out like it makes him feel sick.

Lorenzo looks far from pleased by Marco's interruption.

"I would like to apologise for our late arrival," Marco continues. "An unfortunate misunderstanding had taken place, but not to worry. I will deal with that myself, and as you can see, we are all here now." He gives everyone a moment to look around, letting the "all here now" statement sink in before declaring, "So, let's get this party started, shall we!"

Marco turns to the band, who immediately start playing on his command. The guests, albeit awkwardly, continue with their drinks and dancing. The invited organisation members, I notice, are all either are talking angrily on their phones or frantically texting, panic clearly setting in at how greatly they are outnumbered. Lorenzo seems very calm—too calm. When I look around the room at the Guerra men, they are a force to be reckoned with. An army ready at a moment's notice. Marco does seem to have overdone it though. There must be fifty men here. He likely pulled a lot of them from other jobs in order to get so many here at such short notice.

Shit. That's it. I make my way through the crowds of now drunk civilians.

"Marco. You need to leave."

Marco is talking to my brother, who looks at me like I have gone mad. I'm probably the only person who would dare speak to Marco in public before addressing him as boss.

Marco studies my panicked face. "What is it, Mia?"

"It's a trap. Lorenzo knew you would come. Think about it."

Taking in a deep breath, he looks around the room before looking at me and saying, "There's no trap. But I think it's time we left. We've done what we came to do."

Rolling my eyes, I sigh as Marco turns away from me. At least he's getting out of here, which is exactly what I plan on doing. It's dark outside now, and the air is a lot cooler.

As my car has been taken by the girls, I get my phone out of my bag to call a taxi.

"Need a ride?" Ross is leaning against his unmarked blue BMW police car. He looks like he's been waiting for me.

I think for a moment. But given the presence of the Guerra, along with Marco's warning earlier, I decide to decline. "Thank you, but I'm fine."

Just as I refuse, the wind picks up and sends a shiver down my body. Goosebumps cover my skin, and I instinctively fold my arms to keep warm.

"Come on, it's got heated seats." Ross opens the door invitingly.

None of the Guerra men seem to have noticed me, so I decide to go for it.

"Okay then, Detective. Take me for a ride in your police car."

His smile is wonderful. It makes me feel warm inside. He helps me in like a gentleman and closes the door before sliding into the driver's seat beside me.

"Where would you like to go, princess?"

I laugh. "I am anything but a princess, Ross. But I'm sure a detective like you will have worked that out already. Take me home." I cross my legs, knowing that in doing so, my dress will slide up my thighs, revealing the majority of my legs.

As I expected, Ross's eyes follow the material of my dress. He then sits up awkwardly in his seat, leaning from side to side to make room for the large bulge straining against his trousers. Men are so predictable and easy. I direct Ross to my home and make small talk on the way.

As we pull up my drive, I feel it is best to establish what is going on here.

"To ensure we are both on the same page here," I say confidently, "Tonight is a fuck—nothing more, nothing less."

Ross stops the car immediately, then puts the handbrake on before turning to me with a half smirk, half frown.

"We will go in, have a drink, flirt a little, then sex. No sleeping here, no expectations. This is not and will never be the start of any kind of relationship. Do you understand?"

Ross smiles. He looks almost amused. "I understand perfectly, Mia."

Reaching out to me, he strokes my jaw and guides it towards him. His lips meet mine with gentle pressure, and then he softly glides his tongue between my lips. Something tells me he doesn't actually understand what this is. Well, that's his fault. I finish the kiss and get out of the car. As I walk up the drive, my hips sway with the size of my heels. Ross will definitely have eyes on my arse right now. If he's anything like Marco, my dress will be off as soon as we are inside, and he will be on me.

But to my surprise, Ross accepts the offer of a drink.

"A coffee would be great, thank you."

As I switch the coffee machine on, I feel I may have made a mistake bringing him here. Well, I won't be having a coffee. Opening a bottle of red, I listen to him talk about work. Smiling and nodding, I'm really not interested in what he is saying. He's so handsome, though, so I just enjoy the view, hoping I can telepathically convince him to shut up and fuck me. If it had been Marco, it would all be over by now, and I'd be in bed, feeling completely satisfied and falling asleep with a smile on my face.

A yawn escapes my mouth. No, this is not happening.

I down the last of my wine, stand, then place my glass on the worktop. I remove my dress, and I open Ross's thighs so I can stand in between them. He's still talking to me, although it's much slower, and he isn't making much sense now as his eyes travel up and down my body. Covering his mouth with mine, I press my tongue in to his. I'm hungry for it, but there's something not right, something not quite there.

I bite his tongue a little, and he jumps back, exclaiming, "Ouch."

Seriously, that hurt him? Ignoring it, I continue kissing him. But he doesn't touch me anywhere else. Where's the bum grabbing and boob squeezing? Taking matters into my own hands, I straddle him, pushing my warm core into his groin, and a moan escapes his lips. Finally, we are getting somewhere.

He stands up, holding me in position. "Where is the bedroom?"

"Up the stairs, first door on the right."

To be honest, I'd rather just do it here in the kitchen, but whatever floats his boat. He carefully carries me up the stairs, kissing me gently as he does. It's all a bit too romantic for me. Once we are in the bedroom, he lays me on the bed. I instantly know there is something not right. It's completely dark apart from slight moonlight coming through the blinds. I scan the room as best I can in this light, but everything seems normal.

Trying to ignore it, I concentrate on Ross, who has removed his shirt and tie and is kissing my stomach. It feels nice, but I'd rather just skip to the good part. My stomach flips, and I have butterflies, but it's nothing to do with Ross. I reach toward my bedside light switch, but before I can reach it, the light turns on. The bright ceiling light fills the room. Shielding my eyes with my arm, I give them chance to adjust before I search the room for what I know is there.

Chapter 5

Marco

On the journey home from Lorenzo's party, I get a phone call.

"Boss. The feds are here. Full riot team ready to raid. What should we do?"

"Shit." That Lorenzo bastard. "Can you get out?"

"No, we are completely surrounded," my warehouse manager confirms.

"Usual rules apply. We do not harm law enforcement. Go quietly, and give no comment until I can get a legal team there." I end the call. "Take me back to Lorenzo. I am going to kill him," I fire at Van in the driver's seat.

"Not a chance. I'm taking you home. We need to find out what Lorenzo's end game is. We need to be careful."

As much as I want to rip Lorenzo's head off, I know Van is right. But Lorenzo will get what is coming to him. My mind is buzzing when Van stops the car in front of my house.

"Go and do your shit. Release that anger. I'll check in later."

When I get into my house, I think about going down to my *work* room. There is usually someone down there being taught a lesson they'll never forget—or recover from. But carrying out torture doesn't seem to have the same effect on me anymore. I used to be able to feel the release of tension with each limb I removed or organ I took out. Now it doesn't have the same effect or appeal. No, now there is only one thing that relaxes me, only one thing I can think of doing. I pick up my car keys and head over to Mia's.

My arrangement with Mia started a few years ago, when I was working as an underboss for Leonardo Guerra. We have known each other all our lives.

The status of being a Guerra means that women are readily available to you at all times. But their easiness and eagerness to please soon gets boring. After a drunken night where Mia Alboni ended up in my bed, I realized there is more to sex than just blowing my load. Mia makes me work for her pleasure, and in turn I feel more once I achieve it. Mia had had enough of men wanting more from her, and I definitely didn't want anything more outside of the bedroom, so it seemed like the perfect solution.

I'm already feeling less like a bomb about to explode when I turn into Mia's driveway. That is until I see a car belonging to Detective Rossini.

The anger is now back, but it is joined by something else, another feeling I have not experienced around anyone but Mia. She makes me crazy on another level. We have an arrangement. And that arrangement does not involve detectives.

Mia

"Marco!" I scream over Ross's shoulder.

Ross stops his kissing and looks at me with a frown. "I'm Ross."

Pushing him off me, I storm over to Marco. "What the hell are you doing in my bedroom?"

Marco looks at me with disgust. "Put some clothes on!" he orders.

Oh no, he does not get to break into my home and tell me what to do. Stepping back from him, I unclip my bra. I then slowly let the straps slide down my arms, and my breasts appear in full view. I can see the anger intensifying in Marcos eyes. Marco moves around me, shielding my body from Ross.

"Leave now!" Marco commands to a shocked-looking Ross.

"No. I'm not leaving Mia here with you." Ross stands in front of Marco, trying his best to look brave. Ross is a big, well-built guy. To any regular man, he would look quite threatening. But next to Marco, he may as well be a child.

Recognising the growl coming from deep within Marco, I step in before Ross loses his life. "Please just go, Ross. I am absolutely fine, I promise."

Ross stares at Marco and then back at me. He knows he doesn't have much option, really. Theres no way he could take on Marco.

His shoulders sag and his head bows slightly in defeat. "Okay, but only if you're sure?"

"I am. I will ring you later to check in. Now please just go."

I pick up his shirt and tie and hand them to him as he leaves the room. The second he is out, Marco slams the door with both hands, then he stays there for a moment, his head resting on the door. He growls in anger, and he headbutts the door, banging his fists as he does.

"I told you to stay away from him. Why do you disobey me?!" he says, still standing with his head leaning against the door. He can't look at me.

"You don't own me, Marco. You cannot tell me what to do. How dare you break into my home like this and violate my privacy."

He still doesn't turn around. "He was touching you. Kissing you." His voice gets louder and angrier.

"I'm not listening to this." I make my way to my bathroom.

"Where are you going?"

"For a shower. And you better be gone when I get out."

After slamming the door, I turn the lock quickly so he can't follow me in. I'm so mad with him, I could scream. I rip off my thong and throw it in anger, then get under the steaming shower. The water is slightly too hot, but I don't care. I force my head under and let the heat cover my body in goosebumps. I've let Marco get too close, and now he thinks he can control me. I need to push back. But thought of not being with him again pulls at my insides. This is such a mess. I should have known he would start to control me—or try to, anyway.

"Arrrgh!" I scream in madness, banging the shower screen, causing it to crack. "Shit."

A second later the door crashes open, wrenching from its hinges to fall flat on the bathroom floor. I just look at a Marco and shake my head. Seriously?

"I heard a scream."

Turning away from him without

responding, I grab my shampoo and start to wash my hair. Hopefully if I ignore him, he will go. No such luck. When I open my eyes after finishing my hair care routine, I notice him sitting on my toilet, lid down, head in his hands. After turning off the shower, I wrap myself in a towel and step out in front of him. The bathroom is full of steam and the air is thick.

"What's wrong, Marco?"

It takes him a minute to answer, so I dry myself while I wait. Eventually after a big sigh, he looks up. "You were right. It was a trap."

He stands up and paces up and down my bathroom. Now, my bathroom isn't small, but Marco makes me feel claustrophobic.

"Come into the bedroom."

I take his hand and guide him into my room. My silk robe is on my chair, so I wrap that around me and remove my towel.

Marco continues. "While we were at the event, Lorenzo's men raided the warehouse at the docks as well as the underground casino in town. Nobody saw them coming, and I'd removed all the security and sent them to Villa Mico to that stupid event!"

He's furious, his vein bulges out of his forehead and runs all the way down into his neck. Worrying he might have an aneurysm, I put my hands on his arms and rub gently up and down while I guide him to sit in my chair.

"Why would he do this?" I ponder. "The police and the Guerra have always worked alongside each other. Does he want to start a war?" I'm now pacing up and down. I don't understand. I knew Lorenzo was up to something, but I thought he was trying to cause trouble for us with rival organisations, not this. He has just changed the whole structure of the way the Guerra runs, the way we have worked for generations. This is not good.

"Lorenzo will pay for this. I will make him pay." Marco's body fills my armchair. He looks like a wild beast eager to hunt. Each muscle in his body is tensed and ready to be used to its full potential. I watch him tilt his head from side to side as he cracks his neck. While doing so, his eyes are on mine. He stands up and moves towards me until he is towering above me. "But first, I need to teach you a lesson."

"And what lesson might that be?" I ask, trying to keep my voice as steady as I can, ignoring the fact that my whole body is buzzing with tingles from his words.

"That you belong to me."

"I do not belong to anyone, Marco."

"Oh, but you do. You just haven't realised it yet."

Leaning down, he kisses my neck, grazing my skin with his teeth. In an instant, he has removed my robe before I can even register what he is doing.

Standing back from me, he looks my body up and down. "Just look how your body reacts to me."

I know exactly what he is talking about: goose-pimpled skin, hard nipples.

"And if I dip my finger into your centre, I bet I will find you dripping." He groans his last word.

"It's just sex, Marco," I reply, not believing a word. I hate that it has turned into more. It's not what I wanted.

A smirk crosses his face. "You know that's not true, Mia. Don't you lie to me."

Cupping my face with both hands, he smashes his lips into mine. My mouth opens willingly for him, my knees go weak, and the fireworks of tingling and shivers that only arouse when I'm with Marco begin. He moves his hands lower, massaging my breasts and squeezing my nipples, which sends flushes of heat to my core. He moves both hands to my bum, and cupping my cheeks, he lifts me. My legs automatically go around him. Still kissing him, I move my way up his body so my arms are round his neck.

I can't get enough of him; it seems he feels the same. Our kissing is desperate. We are hungry for each other. His hands are in my hair, holding my head to his mouth. I couldn't stop if I wanted to. He backs me up against the wall, knocking a picture off in the process. Our bodies grind into each other of their own accord. It's like an instinct that takes over when we are together.

"I need you. I need more of you," I gasp.

Not needing to ask him twice, I am spun around and thrown onto my bed, where I lie completely naked in front of Marco, who is still, to my disappointment, fully dressed.

"Open wide for me," he instructs.

"Take off your clothes," I push back.

Marco rips open his shirt, losing a few buttons in the process, and discards it onto the floor. "Now open," he pleads, but I cross my legs.

"Trousers too. I want to see all of you."

With a growl and a scowl, he quickly removes his remaining clothing. Without warning he dives onto the bottom of the bed. He grabs me by the ankles and slides me down towards him. I laugh in surprise. He has a mischievous look on his face.

"I said, open." Marco opens my legs with my ankles, his face diving in-between them. His tongue slips through my centre, and he rubs his bearded chin on my clitoris, making my body jump with the sensitive pleasure. "This is mine. Tell me this is mine," Marco demands, but the pleasure I feel is so intense, I can't speak.

His tongue works gently, lapping at my core, then he presses his bearded mouth against me, massaging round and around, giving the most pleasurable friction. Then, before it gets too much, his tongue is back, and the whole process starts again. I'm in heaven. My legs start to shake and my body bucks with intense pleasure. Just as I'm going over the edge, it stops.

Marco leans over me. "Tell me it's mine."

"It's yours." I would literally agree to anything right now.

Marco squints at me, he doesn't fully believe me. I feel him line himself up, and he swipes his tip up through my centre, coating himself in my arousal. I open my legs, ready for the fulfilling pleasure about to begin.

Staring into my eyes, he says, "You belong to me." As he speaks, he thrusts, opening, stretching, and filling me.

My mouth opens with a moan of pleasure, and the look of joy on Marcos's face pulls at my chest. Putting my hands around his head, I pull him to me, our lips crashing together again, consuming each other's moan of passion. My legs wrap around him—it's like I can't get close enough. I need more of him. He thrusts and thrusts, his tip rubbing against that glorious spot deep inside me.

"More, I need more," I gasp into his mouth.

Taking my bottom lip between his teeth, he pulls our mouths away from each other. I'm missing his lips immediately, but then he puts my legs over his shoulders, and… "Oh yes, that's it."

He is inside me to the brim, his pubic bone creating the friction I need to tip me over the edge. It builds, and I cry out.

"Look at me!" he orders.

I see the euphoria on his face. He pounds with force. He's like an animal, and I absolutely love it.

"Now!" he bellows.

Our moans and groans and cries of pleasure surely will be heard from outside, but I don't care. I'm in another world, a place of extreme pleasure where I have only ever been with Marco—a I place where only he and I exist. Our bodies buck and shake in the aftermath. The sounds coming from Marco in his pleasure fill me with joy. I could get off from his noises alone.

Relaxing into my bed, I close my eyes, enjoying the satisfaction my whole body feels. Waiting for Marco to remove himself, I'm surprised to feel him kissing my feet. Opening my eyes, I see Marco holding my feet still propped on his shoulders, kissing my soles with his eyes closed. Something quite intimate that he has never done before. I lay still for a moment, watching him. Taking a deep breath with his last kiss, he savours the smell of my feet. I'm glad I have just showered. A smile I don't see often fills his face. He puts my big toe in his mouth and sucks hard, making a loud poppng sound as he releases.

"From the tips of your toes..." He kisses along my shin and up to my thigh. "... all the way..." He continues kissing up my body until he reaches the top of my head, where he lingers with a bigger kiss. "... to the top of your head...." He then brings his nose to touch mine, our eyes connected. "Is mine!" he booms, giving me one last thrust before he pulls out and walks to the bathroom.

The reminder of our passion leaks from between my legs a feeling I'm not used to.

"I'll get the doctor to prescribe you the morning-after pill, you don't want to be seen in the chemist" he shouts as he closes the door.

I roll my eyes as I get up and follow him in.

Chapter 6

Mia

"I can sort myself out, thank you," I say as I also make a mental reminder to get myself checked out. I have no idea what Marco gets up to. I am on the pill, but I've never not used protection before.

Sitting on the toilet while I wait for him to shower, I admire Marco's body. He fills the space with such masculinity. Every muscle in his body is trying to escape from his skin. His body pretty much covered with hair, which on any other man I'd find repulsive. His olive skin is scattered with scars, which only adds to his dangerous demeanour that I cannot resist.

"Are you done yet?" I stand impatiently in front of him.

He opens the glass door and pulls me in before I have chance to protest.

"Oh no, little lady—I am far from done." He spins me round. "Hands on the wall in front of you!"

I do as I'm told.

"Lower and spread those legs."

As soon as I do, I'm thrust into the air because of his height. I think I'm going headfirst into the wall, but he catches me, holding my weight as he pounds. He holds me as if I weigh nothing. The feeling is incredible.

"All mine!" he growls and then groans.

Amazingly, considering we have only just climaxed, it doesn't take either of us long to come again.

As we finish, he sets me on my feet, puts this large hand around my throat, and lowers his mouth to my ear. "I don't want to have to tell you again. This body is mine."

"We will see." I swiftly duck and remove myself from his grip around my throat, elbowing him in the stomach as do. "Now get out of my shower. I need to wash again."

With a grunt, he leaves as I lather myself in shower gel.

When I return to my bedroom, I don't expect to see Marco in my bed and under the covers, scrolling through his phone.

"What the hell are doing?" I spit in disbelief.

"I'm staying here tonight," he says without looking up from his phone.

"Oh no, you're not. I sleep alone," I retort,

storming over to my dresser. I put on a vest top and pants. When he doesn't reply, I find my phone and leave the room.

"Where are you going?" he bellows after me.

"I'm sleeping in the spare room." I quickly shut the door of my guestroom and flick the lock.

He tries the handle. "Open this door now," he instructs.

"No, Marco. You are not the boss of me."

"Correction. I am the boss. Now open this fucking door!" He bangs his fist against it.

Ignoring him, I get in to bed and open the CCTV on the sanctuary to check on the animals.

A loud bang echoes through the house as Marco knocks the door from its hinges. Without saying a word, he scoops me up and carries me back into my bedroom, then places me on my bed. I huff, folding my arms. Realising I'm not going to win this argument, I pull the covers over me, turning away from him. He gets in beside me and turns out the light.

"Sleep, little lady. You get grumpy when you're tired."

I'm so annoyed, I can't sleep. Marco doesn't have that problem. I know this, as I can hear him snoring. I decide to get up and physically go to check on my animals.

It's the early hours of the morning, so the sanctuary is pretty quiet. I carefully disarm the alarm and let myself in, trying not to disturb the night staff. There are generally one or two of the staff that stay overnight just to make sure the animals are okay. I go into the lounge first, where there are a few cats and dogs nestled cosily on the sofas. A couple lift their heads to see who has entered before they return to their slumber. I pop my head into the bedroom because I can't help myself. Sophie, one of the staff, looks up from her snooze, noticing me enter. I give her a little wave to let her know everything is fine. It's not unusual that I would come here in the middle of the night. The room is filled with cute little dog snores. In the dim glow of the night lights, I see the puppies snuggling up to their mum. I close the door and leave them to sleep and go into the kitchen, where I find Mabel, one of our eldest staff members. She's sat bottle feeding one of our latest rescues, a kitten who was found alone in a shed, very malnourished and full of fleas.

"How's she doing? I ask, making her jump.

"Oh Mia, you gave me fright." She chuckles, standing up to come towards me. "She's doing just great. All the fleas have gone, and she has put on weight. Here, have a look at her." Mabel hands me the tiny grey kitten.

"Aww, she's gorgeous. You've done a great job with her. Thank you, Mabel. Another few weeks and she will be ready for her forever home." The kitten wriggles in my arms, obviously trying to get back to Mabel, so I hand her back.

"I've been thinking about that, Mia, and wondered whether it would be okay if I kept her. I'd make a donation to the sanctuary, obviously—"

I cut her off. "I think that's a wonderful idea, Mabel. She loves you already. No donation necessary, and any vet bills, you charge to me, okay?"

Mabel's face lights up. "Thank you, Mia, so much."

Pottering about the kitchen, I make us a cup of coffee, making small talk with Mabel, until I see her demeanour change.

"What's wrong, Mabel?"

She is looking towards the window, squinting. It's dark outside, but we have lights around the premises. "I think I just saw someone climb over the fence."

Remembering I have disarmed the alarms, I go straight to my safe and get out my gun. "Stay here. I'll go and check it out."

After quietly opening the side door, I sneak out, keeping my back to the wall and my gun in front of me I make my way around the building. It's deadly silent apart from the odd bat flying overhead. The gardens are clear, and so are the outhouses. When I get to the front, I sense a presence. As I hold my gun in front of me, ready to fire, my arm is grabbed and twisted around my back, my gun is taken from my hand, my back is held against their body, and I'm pushed through the front door.

Chapter 7

Mia

"What have I told you about playing with guns, little lady?" Marco whispers into my ear.

"What the hell!" I pull out of his hold and smack him in the chest with both hands.

"What the hell are you doing out at this time? I woke up and you were gone. What is this place?" He looks around him. A few of the dogs have heard the commotion and have come to see what's going on.

"This is my sanctuary. I've told you about the animals I rescue." I have mentioned it in passing, but it isn't something I like to speak about with the Guerra.

"I thought you had a few kennels with dogs in them, not this."

The dogs have started barking at the uninvited visitor, which has alerted most of the other dogs, who have now woken up and come to investigate. Most of them stand back, barking and growling at him. I'm worried about Marco's reaction. If he doesn't approve of this, he could make things very difficult for me. He'd have a fight on his hands if tried to interfere.

One of our more confident animals, a little chihuahua with three legs, runs straight through the crowd of dogs now gathering, and barks at Marco's feet. I wince, knowing that one kick from Marco would end this cheeky girl's life. I've seen firsthand how cruel Guerra men can be to animals. But he surprises me. After staring at her for a few seconds, he bends his knees and holds his hand out for her to sniff. The chihuahua has a smell and decides she likes him, so then proceeds to climb up Marco's leg and onto his lap. I laugh as Marco smiles at the little dog and sits himself on the floor, allowing the dog to climb up his shirt and kiss his face. The rest of the dogs see this as an invitation to do the same, and soon Marco is covered in dogs. I sit down beside him, and we laugh as we give out as many ear scratches and cuddles as we can. Once the excitement is over, the dogs wander off, returning to their beds or going in search of food. Apart from one. The chihuahua is curled up on Marco's lap while he strokes her.

"It looks like Tipsy has taken quite a fancy to you."

"Tipsy?" Marco's face is horrified at the name.

"Yes, Tipsy. With only having three legs, she waddles around like she's had one too many vodkas."

"What happened to her?" Marco studies her fur, noticing all her scars.

"She was used as bait to train fighting dogs and left for dead. Her leg had been completely ripped off."

Marco's face is murderous as he listens.

"We didn't think she would make it, but here she is, full of personality. She's been through so much, and yet she's such a lovely temperament. We've not had much luck in rehoming her, but we love her to bits, and she's happy here."

Marco doesn't say anything. He just continues to study her.

"I'll go and check everything is all right, and then we can go back to the house."

After I have made sure Mabel and Sophie have everything under control, I return to find Marco still cuddling Tipsy.

"Come on, let's go, *boss*," I joke.

Marco looks at me with a grin. "See, now you're getting it," he chirps.

"Ha, I don't think so." I hold out my arms to take Tipsy, but he doesn't pass her to me.

He stands up with her tucked under his arm.

"She's had a stressful night. I think it would be best if we take her back to the house with us," Marco states firmly as he opens the door and walks out of the building.

I shake my head in disbelief, and I can't help the smile that fills my face.

In the morning I wake to find Marco sitting in the chair, talking softly to Tipsy.

"You're a beautiful girl—yes, you are."

I try and hold in my laugh, but Marco looks up and stops talking immediately. He stands up and passes her to me on the bed. He is already fully dressed. "You will have to look after her today. I have work to do."

I laugh at his comment. "So, what's the plan?" I ask, remembering the situation from last night.

Marco looks at me for a moment, clearly thinking over how much to tell me. I can read him like a book.

"Under Lorenzo's instruction, sixteen members of the Guerra have been arrested and questioned over illegal gambling, drug trafficking, and holding illegal weapons. The entire legal team is working on it, but it doesn't look good." Marco fiddles with his tie in the mirror.

"So, what are you going to do?"

"Take matters into my own hands. Lorenzo is going to wish he never laid eyes on me."

I dread to think what that means. I pick Tipsy up and make my way out of the bedroom.

"Do you want a coffee before you go?" I call back to Marco, feeling stunned by my words. Marco in my home is very surreal.

"No, I need to go. But there's surprise on the kitchen table for you. Be careful when you open it."

A surprise? Marco has never got me anything before. Feeling a little bit excited, I go into the kitchen and let Tipsy outside. I see a large black box on the table. It's very heavy and well sealed. I get some scissors and open the top. Inside, there's a vacuumed-packed plastic bag containing what looks like some sort of skin. Feeling nervous about what it is, I carefully lift it out of the box. Is it a dead pig? Blood saturates the inside of the package.

"Urgh!" I drop it and jump back, crashing into Marco's chest. He holds me upright. "What the hell is that?"

"Does the name John Wince mean anything to you?"

I think for a moment. "It rings a bell, but I'm not sure why."

"John Wince was the organiser of the Wince dog fighting organisation. That is his leg."

"Bloody hell, Marco, get that thing out of here."

"Someone will be round to collect it later." Marco walks over to the door and lets Tipsy in. "I'm having it skinned so all the dogs can gnaw at the bone." He strokes his new best friend and then leaves the house.

I'm stuck on the spot, unable to move, my mouth agape.

Chapter 8

Marco

I've been going over the options all night, and there is only one solution. He is trying to take me down, so I do one better. Starting with getting my men out of jail, which can't be done legally.

Van arrives to pick me up from my house. I drove back in plenty of time to not arouse suspicion. Although who I fuck is my business, I do have a lot of respect for Van. But I need to understand what exactly is happening with his sister before anyone else finds out.

"Boss." Van nods at me through the review mirror when I get in the back seat. "The team are at the house, waiting for the go-ahead. There are six armed police officers with two dogs."

"Bring them all in. Shoot to stop, not to kill. And no harm must come to the dogs." The car suddenly comes to a stop.

Van eyeballs me through the mirror. "Did you say no harm to the dogs?"

"Yes, Van. Are you going deaf? Shoot to stop,

not to kill. And no harm must come to the dogs."

Van raises his eyebrows with wide eyes, then continues to drive.

"The more hostages the better. We will need the names of each officer and their family contacts. Let's hope they all have wives and children."

"Should we bring the dogs as hostages as well?" Van asks.

"Stop with all the fucking dog talk. What do you not understand? Leave the dogs there. Don't touch the fucking dogs."

Van briefly raises his hands in the air in apology before returning them to the steering wheel. I cannot be dealing with bullshit today. We sit in silence for the rest of the drive. It takes about forty minutes. When we pull up, I see my men stood outside the door to the office building. More of my men are bringing out police officers one by one.

"He's on the top floor, boss."

Not replying, I make my way inside and go up the four flights of stairs. When I reach the top floor, I can see Lorenzo through the glass door, sitting at his desk. His eyes are on me. He has the look of his own death on his face.

"Mr. Guerra, you're making a big mistake. If you kill me, you will still be in the same position.

The whole police force and Italian intelligence agencies are on to you now. There is no going back. You're just making everything ten times worse for yourself."

Letting him blabber on in fear, I walk around the office. Boxes of files line the floors, along with piles of paperwork and evidence bags.

"Did you think I wouldn't find you here?" I say, picking up a file and flicking through the pages.

"I didn't think you would be stupid enough to look for me," Lorenzo responds.

Throwing the file on the floor, I stare at him. "You have forty-eight hours, Lorenzo. Make all this disappear."

Lorenzo laughs. "I don't think so, Guerra. I am going to be the one that finally brings you down." His face wears a cocky smirk.

"Well, in that case, you won't be the only one who disappears. Forty-eight hours. Starting from now."

As I make my way out of the room, I hear his phone ring. A few seconds later, I hear him screaming my name, followed by obscenities and the noise of furniture hitting the walls.

When I get to the bottom of the stairs, Van is waiting for me.

"We have Lorenzo's wife and sons in

custody," he informs me. "There were three police casualties, and the others are also being transported to the warehouse. And you will be pleased to know no dogs were harmed in the making of this operation. Some of our men, however, have nasty dog-related injuries."

"They'll survive."

Van rolls his eyes at me while opening the door to my car. "The rest of the operations have also gone well. We have everyone on the list as well as a few extras," Van explains before closing my door behind me.

"Extras?"

"Yes. I thought the Prime Minister might also be useful." Van looks smug as he climbs into the driver's seat.

"Not a bad idea." I nod and pull my phone out to check on Mia. I've had her home security system installed on my phone. For safety reasons, obviously.

She's still at home. Her car is parked in the driveway. Just as I'm about to click onto the internal cameras, I see her appear from the front door, wearing a red trouser suit that hugs those delicious curves. Her long dark hair is in curls and swishes when she walks. Unable to take my eyes off her, I watch as she gets into her convertible. She turns her car around and heads down the drive. The men I have guarding her pull out and follow behind her. Mia's car suddenly comes to a stop. Her door swings open, and she charges up to the car following her. She opens the door and pulls out the driver. A laugh escapes my mouth.

I notice Van watching me curiously through his mirror. Wishing the cameras had sound, I try to imagine what she is saying to them. Mia looks angry, waving her arms around. After a minute or so, she returns to her car, but it doesn't move. The image then disappears with an incoming call. Mia.

"Mia, to what do I owe the pleasure?"

Van stares at me curiously through the mirror, no doubt confused by the amused smirk on my face as I answer my phone to speak with his sister.

"Call your men off now. I do not need babysitting," she snaps into the phone.

"They are there for your protection only, Mia."

"No, you are spying on me, trying to control me. Call them off, Marco, or I swear I won't let you touch me ever again."

I turn the volume down on my phone, making sure Van cannot hear his sister's outburst.

"The Guerra are under attack, Mia. Do not make things more difficult than they already are. Either stay with your security, or do not leave your house." Ending the call, I look at Van, who's staring at me with interest.

"Your sister is a difficult woman."

Van doesn't reply, just puts his eyes on the road. The screen again fills with Mia, so I watch as she returns to her car in a strop. She leaves with the security following her. I make a mental note to have a camera installed in her car. Again, just for protection.

I was so lost in my thoughts, I hadn't realised my car had come to stop.

"We're here, boss."

I get out without a word. This particular warehouse has an underground club. The police have no idea this is even here, let alone connected with us. The club will be closed while we house the hostages. We enter through the concealed door. Van leads the way down the stairs to the staff quarters.

"I'll speak to the Prime Minister first."

The Prime Minister is brought to my office.

"Mr. Prime Minister, please take a seat."

"Mr. Guerra, what is all this about?" The Prime Minister takes a seat, putting his hands together on his lap.

"For generations, the Guerra have ruled the cities through business, not bloodshed. Granted, the way we carry out justice isn't the way the police force would, but we keep the streets in order. We do not tolerate disrespect, only loyalty. We pay taxes—taxes that fund this country and your government."

The Prime Minister nods in agreement.

"Lorenzo has disregarded our unwritten agreement, our legacy. You must understand, Mr. Prime Minister, Lorenzo is creating a war between the police and the Guerra, which in turn means I am at war with the government. And I can assure you, I will win that war. The Guerra will stop paying any taxes. Investments in government projects will stop. Crime will soar, protection will cease, favours will stop."

"I can assure *you*, Mr. Guerra, this is the last thing I, or the government, want."

"I bet it's not," I agree, remembering the large coverup the Guerra did for him and his peers just last month. "He has forty-eight hours. You may stay in my office and use my phone. Sort it out, Prime Minister, or you'll be my first example."

Nodding his head in agreement, the man looks white as a ghost.

"Van will stay here while you make your calls," I state, then leave them to it.

I want to check on the hostages. Lorenzo's family are in one of the private lounges. They seem comfortable and as relaxed as can be expected under the circumstances. As long as Lorenzo sees sense, they will come to no harm.

Chapter 9

Marco

The police are all in the bar area. Each of them has their hands behind them in their own handcuffs—that's Van's little quirk. He thinks restraining them with their own equipment is hilarious. They don't look as relaxed as Lorenzo's family. Some of them are terrified, sat on their own, heads down and trying not to make eye contact with anyone, while others are huddled in groups, trying the play the heroes by quietly plotting their escape or takeover, thinking we don't know what they are up to.

A few of my men enter the room with plates of food for the hostages. They lay them down on the tables.

"Eat. But if I see anyone eating like animals straight from the dish, I will lock you in a cage and treat you like an animal," one of them instructs. The hostages look at each other in disbelief.

"Are you going to uncuff us, then?"

"No," another of my men says as he lays

a bunch of metre-long canes with plastic spoons attached to the ends next to the plates. "We know how many of these there are. If any are missing when we collect them, you will each lose that amount of fingers."

My men then leave the room, laughing. I keep watching through the one-way glass window, interested to see how it unfolds. This technique is a good way of finding out who we need to keep our eye on and possibly split from the rest of the group as well as who will be mostly likely to crack under pressure and give us information we need. As expected, voices are raised and tempers grow, but eventually one clever dick realises that they can hold the cane at their back, spoon on some food and feed someone else. My men will be watching the cameras and assessing each hostage.

Once I have made sure everything is under control, I leave.

Knowing Mia's location, I find her in a coffee shop in town.

"Make that two," I demand over her shoulder as she orders her coffee.

Mia doesn't turn around to greet me, but I see her reflection in the coffee machine in front of her. She rolls her eyes with pouty lips. We make our way to the end of the queue in silence. When I try and pay for both our drinks, she bats my hand away.

It's not until I join her at a table that she speaks to me.

"Marco, what are you doing here?"

"I'm having a coffee. What are you doing here?"

"This is getting ridiculous. You're acting like some kind of stalker. Haven't you got something better to do?"

"Oh, there's definitely something better I'd rather be doing." I lean back in my chair and give her a wink.

Mia scowls at me, but I can see she's fighting a smile.

"You will go to dinner with me tonight."

"No, I won't. I am busy tonight."

"Who with?" I demand. She better not be seeing that weasel Ross again.

Leaning back in her chair and folding her arms, she replies, "That's none of your business."

Feeling myself harden, I move in my seat to get more comfortable. I need to pound that attitude right out of her.

Seeing my frustration, she sighs and continues. "I have my training session with Max tonight."

"I don't like Max. I will do your defence training from now on."

"Don't be absurd. Max is one of your men, and he's the best fighter you have."

My blood boils, but it's true. Out of all my men, Max is the only one who would have a chance at taking me down. That being said, the thought of him putting his hands on Mia fills me with range.

"Mia, you will do as I say. I will train you from now on."

Mia stands, placing her hands on the table as she leans down to me. "No. I have had enough now, Marco. Stay out of my way, stay out of my bed, and stay out of my life. I am done." And she leaves the coffee shop.

Full of rage, I throw the table on its side. The whole of the room falls silent and looks at me.

"What are you all looking at?!" I boom.

On exiting, I see her tottering down the street. Knowing my guards are watching her, I go back to my car to calm down.

Chapter 10

Mia

I knew this would happen. It's my own fault for letting him into my bed. I should have kicked him out. I'm so furious during my drive, I don't even know how I've got home. Pulling into my driveway, I notice Max is already here for our training session. I go inside, and after quickly changing into my gym top and shorts, I enter my workout room, where Max has already laid the mats out on the floor.

"Mia, great, you're here. Okay, let's start off with the usual warmup, then we will carry on with where we left off last week."

Tonight's session is intense. The punch bag gets its stuffing knocked out of it, and Max ends up with a bleeding nose.

"I'm so sorry, Max. I don't know what happened. I got carried away."

"Don't worry, I have had much worse. You've been great tonight—powerful and extremely quick to react. You even caught me off guard."

My heart is racing, and I'm sweating head to toe. I've just about gotten rid of my frustration when I see Marco standing in the doorway.

"I think I'm done for today. Thanks, Max."

Max throws me my towel and holds his hand out for a high five.

"Same time next week. Be careful, Mia." He nods towards Marco.

"I'll be fine. I can handle him." I smile.

After greeting Marco, Max leaves.

I walk straight past Marco in the doorway and head upstairs and put the shower on.

"Mia, will you come to dinner with me, please?"

I can hear the strain in this voice. He's not used to asking nicely for people to do things.

"No, and get out of my bathroom."

Marco steps further in and closes the door behind him.

"Arrghh! Why are you so impossible?"

Smirking, he puts the lid down on my toilet and takes a seat. The toilet seat makes a loud cracking sound before the it buckles under his weight, causing him to fall to the side. He quickly catches himself, and I can't but help laugh. He stands up and looks at what he's done, then rips off the broken top, leaving just the seat.

"I'll get a new one fitted tomorrow," he grumbles,

"Just leave before you do any more damage."

"I'm not going anywhere until you agree to have dinner with me."

"Why? Why, Marco, is it so important that I have dinner with you tonight?"

Rubbing his bristled jaw with his hand, he answers. "Lorenzo has something else up his sleeve. I'm sure of it. You have an intuition about these things."

"Let me get this straight. You, the head of the Guerra, want a woman's help."

"No, not help. A discussion, with you," he disagrees firmly.

Marco looks troubled. He isn't his usual together self.

"Fine, but get out of my house so I can get ready. Pick me up in an hour."

In one hour exactly, Marco knocks on my front door. I'm ready and waiting, so I open the door immediately. Greeted with a side view of Marco while he checks our surroundings, I take in his appearance. He looks incredibly handsome tonight. His hair and beard have been freshly cut, and his facial hair accentuates his square jawline.

Wearing his usual attire of a custom-fit black suit, he somehow looks different tonight. Maybe it's the large gin and tonic I had while I was getting ready.

When he does turn to me, his eyes are wide. "You look incredible, Mia."

A blush fills my face and I feel a little surprised by my reaction.

"Oh, this old thing." I brush off his compliment and walk around him to the car. Feeling his eyes on my new skintight leather skirt and red corset top, I hear a growl sound from within him, which makes me smile. "I take it we are going in the Ferrari?" When I spin round to look at him, his eyes are on my bum.

Smirking, he moves his eyes up to mine. "You like red and power. I thought you'd appreciate it."

That I do. He opens the door for me, and I climb into the beautiful interior. As we set off down the driveway, I notice the guards following behind us in their SUV.

As soon as we leave the driveway, Marco accelerates. The G-force instantly pushes my whole body against the soft leather seat. The roar of the engine vibrates through every part of me. Butterflies of excitement build in my stomach. Marco has never looked so powerful. If I could physically get out of my seat, I would devour him right now. Catching me looking at him, his face turns primal.

"Hold that thought. There will be plenty of time for that later," he groans.

Marco parks right in front of the restaurant doors, over the yellow no-parking lines, because why wouldn't he. The two guards assigned to me appear behind us. They enter the restaurant while we wait outside, and once they have made sure it's clear, they hold the doors open for us.

"I'll take it from here," Marco instructs as he waves them away and puts his hand on the small of my back to lead me inside.

The restaurant is busy, but we are lead through to the private dining area in the back. Heads turn and watch us walk through the restaurant.

The private area is dimly lit with lots of candles. Classical music plays quietly in the background.

"This is all very romantic, Marco. I thought this was to discuss business?"

"It is. This is just how the private room is."

"That's a relief. I had visions of you getting down on one knee," I joke.

Marco just stares at me, clearly not finding it funny.

Once we have ordered and I have my glass of

wine, Marco begins to talk about Lorenzo. "There's something else that I just can't put my finger on."

"How do you mean?" I inquire, as I have my own thoughts on this too.

"He must have known what our reaction would be after the raids. Of course we would retaliate."

"I agree."

"So, what do you think his endgame is?" Annoyance fills his face as he swirls the ice around his glass of whiskey.

"It could be several things. But what he will want is power and control. Which you have. We need to keep our eyes open for anything out of the ordinary. What is currently going on could all still be a distraction. Something to take your attention off what is really happening. But then again, he could just be that stupid and thought he could legally take down the Guerra."

"Maybe, but my gut is telling me otherwise." After downing the last of his drink, he presses the buzzer for the waiter.

He comes in immediately with a fresh round of drinks.

"You need to be careful, Marco. You need extra protection. Get more guards for yourself."

"I can protect myself, and I have Van."

Rolling my eyes, I pick up my fresh glass of wine. It's cold, crisp, and fruity, and it's going to my head. "Please, Marco. Just until this with Lorenzo is over."

"I'll speak to Van." He dismisses that conversation and changes the subject to my animals.

While we eat our dinner, I update Marco on the dogs' latest antics and my future plans for the sanctuary. It's strange how comfortable and easy it is to speak to Marco. I have known Marco all my life, but we've spoken more in these past couple of hours than we have in our lifetime. Funny how you can know someone all this time but never really know them at all. He's actually got a good sense of humour.

While Marco settles the bill, I visit the ladies' room. Sitting and doing my business, I think about my evening with Marco. Something has changed between us. It's hard to believe the man I have just had dinner with is the same man I have seen disembowel men with his bare hands.

I'm just finishing up when I hear the door open and the quiet sobs of a woman. As I'm unlocking the door, a man enters the bathroom.

"Sarah!" he shouts, along with a lot of obscenities.

Deciding I don't want to walk out into the middle of a domestic, I hang back for a moment, hoping they will take their argument outside. But listening to the man criticise and verbally attack this woman who just continues to break her heart has me furious.

As I open the door of my cubical, the man has his fist raised about to hit the woman. Obviously used to this kind of attack, the woman covers her face with her hands. Bolting out, I grab the man's fist before it makes contact. Twisting the man's arm around his back, I kick the inside of his knee so he buckles to the floor. The weasel of a man cries out in pain.

Still holding his arm to the brink of dislocation, I pull his hair with my other hand, bringing his ear to my mouth. "Don't you ever hurt a woman."

"Who the fuck are you?" he spits.

Dragging him up by his hair and arm, I smash his nose into the sink before lifting his head to look at me through the mirror. "My name is Mia Alboni, and I am your worst nightmare."

I let him drop to the floor, then stand on his balls with my stilettos. His scream can no doubt be heard for miles.

In the mirror, I see Marco in the doorway, leaning against door frame. He's got his arms folded and a very satisfied smile on his face.

"I came to see if you needed a hand, but

I see you have everything under control." There's amusement in his voice. "Come on, I better get you home before you cause any more trouble."

As I leave with Marco, I hear the man mutter under his breath. "Bitch."

Marco obviously hears him, too, as he spins straight around to re-enter the bathroom. He picks him up by his neck and slams his face into the mirror. Holding it into the broken glass, he calmly explains, "Nobody insults a Guerra, and nobody insults my woman."

The sink breaks with the force of the man's head. If he would have just kept his mouth shut and let us leave, he would still be alive. But Marco cannot let the Guerra be disrespected, no matter how small the insult.

Once Marco has ordered the cleanup, we get back in the Ferrari. I feel instantly excited as soon as my body sinks into the seat, the roar of the engine vibrating through my core. Marco wears a proud expression as he puts his foot down, setting off on our way. Once again, the G-force pushes me further into my seat. I put my hand on Marco's large thigh, gently squeezing in anticipation. Sexual tension builds between us. He again accelerates.

We are on a long stretch of tree-lined road, and it's late, so there are no other cars on it. The odd streetlamp and moonlight give just enough light to see the curves ahead.

"I love this car," I admit.

"I love you in this car," he replies as he slams on the brakes, almost giving me whiplash.

"What are you doing?" I ask as he pulls off to the side of the road.

"I can't wait any longer."

Dragging my head towards him, he slams his lips against mine. He's desperate for me, and me for him.

Chapter 11

Mia

"Get out," Marco instructs as he opens his door.

He rounds the car to open my door. He takes my hand and leads me to the front, where he turns me so I'm facing away from him towards the car.

"Put your hands on the bonnet."

Leaning down, I place the palms of my hands on the shiny red paintwork to either side of the little yellow badge emblazoned with a black horse. Marco places his hands on my bum and squeezes. He then grinds into me. I feel how hard and ready for me he is. He then unzips my skirt and lets it drop to the ground. I step out of it as he instructs.

His mouth goes to my shoulder, kissing hungrily, biting gently. "Spread your legs." His fingers swipe between my legs.

"I'm so ready for you," I admit.

Understanding my need, he unzips his

trousers. I then feel the glorious tip at my entrance. Looking up, I see our reflection in the windscreen. My eyes meet Marco's in the glass, and I see a look of desire on his face. He winks and pushes in with all his power, his hands braced on my hips to ensure he fills me to the brim.

Nothing beats that first feeling of being opened and filled, that first stretch, the tingles and rush that ripple through your body. My moans are uncontrollable. My screams of pleasure combine with his groans, echoing into the night. Both of us watch our reflection. It's an image I plan to store in my memory forever. This alpha of a man receiving pleasure from my body, the full moon behind him, the trees surrounding us, the powerful red car beneath my hands.

It doesn't take long for the whole experience to make my screams louder and my body convulse around him. Marco is tipped over the edge by my ecstasy, roars from deep within him echoing into the night. I watch him, mesmerised, grateful my body can do this to a man as beautiful as him. He looks incredible, the moonlight accentuating his chiselled face. He is the epitome of an alpha male and a sex god.

On the drive home, Marco takes it a bit slower. Both of us feeling satisfied, we enjoy the sound and motion of the car. It's really been an incredible night.

"I've got an early start in the morning, so no sleepovers."

Marco groans in disappointment. "Why, where are you going?" he demands.

"I'm going to London. I have a new makeup range launching in one of the big department stores."

"No. You can't leave the country while we have a situation. I can't leave. I am needed here."

"You are not invited, anyway. The girls and I are going for one night. The issue is here in Italy. I'll be perfectly safe in England."

"I'm not happy about this. Why didn't you mention it earlier?"

"You are not my keeper, Marco. Stop trying to control me."

He pulls the car into my driveway. I open my door and get out as soon as we come to a stop.

"Mia, get back here! I haven't finished talking to you yet."

"Well, I have finished with you. Go home, Marco."

I storm into my house and slam my door. After kicking my heels off and throwing my bag down, I go straight up to bed. Just as I let my guard down, the beast comes raging back.

Lucia and Marisa arrive at 5:00 a.m. I hear their excited laughter as they walk up the drive, dragging their Louis Vuitton suitcases behind them. They both scream when I open the door, then discard their luggage and run to greet me.

"Hi, girls. Ready for our trip?"

The guards pick up their discarded bags and load them into the back of the SUV. Looks like they will also be accompanying us. But as long as they stay out of our way, I don't mind, as it will keep Marco off my back at least.

We fly first-class to London City Airport. The girls take full advantage of the free drinks. I go over my speech for the event and make sure I have memorised the names of the people I need to thank and mention.

We check in to the King Hotel in Trinity Square, which is just around the corner from the event. The guards check out the security while us girls freshen up and get changed.

"Mia, you look stunning," Lucia squeals when I come out of the bathroom.

"Damn, you look so hot!" Marisa agrees. "All eyes will be on you tonight."

"Well, that's the plan." I've got to admit, this dress is pretty eye-catching. It's a short, tight, strapless dress. Red, of course, and covered in jewels and sequins. Not the most comfortable thing to wear, a little scratchy, but no pain no gain.

"Let's make a toast." Marsia pops open a bottle of champagne. "To Mia, the best friend a girl could wish for, and to MIA, the best and biggest makeup brand in the world. To Mia."

We all clink glasses and down them in one.

"Right, girls—let's go make some money."

I really hope tonight goes as well as I want. I'm hoping that after the launch, my brand will have the biggest net worth in the world. Over the years I have had many companies wanting to buy my name, and I have always said no. But I feel I have taken my business as far as I wanted now. I'm ready to sell—for the right price. My heart isn't in it anymore. It's all about my sanctuary. I'm so proud of what I have achieved on my own, but I think I am done with it all now.

First, we go to the department store to officially open the new range of cosmetics. We are taken by limousine. It pulls up outside one of the entrances, which has been made exclusive to our event. There are crowds of people gathered behind rope barriers and a red carpet lining the floor. The guards see us in, not letting anyone get near us. Frustrated as I am for them not letting me speak to anyone, I keep my cool with a big smile firmly on my face. We are greeted by the organiser and the director of the department store.

"Mia, it is such a pleasure to finally meet you," says the organiser, who looks genuinely excited to see me.

Thankfully I memorised both of their names on the plane ride over and have learnt just enough about them to make small talk as we make our way to the cosmetic department.

"I really hope you like what we have done with the displays. We've worked with your designers really closely for months. We've never had anything quite this spectacular before," the director says to me as we reach the MIA area.

I'm drawn in as soon as I see it. Marisa and Lucia scream in excitement, walking faster in front of me to get a better look. There's a row of makeup stations with LED lights around the mirrors. Everything glitters and sparkles. Each display has what looks like a mirror on the side but is really an interactive AI that shows what your face will look like with each one of our products, kind of like hairstyle apps but for makeup. It's the latest technology and cost me a fortune, but hopefully it will pay off.

The event is invitation only. The guests have arrived and are let in to have a look around. There are canapes and champagne for everyone to enjoy while they watch demonstrations from some of our makeup artists. We selected the guests specifically for our own gain. There are bloggers and influencers, celebrities with big social media followings, magazine editors, and of course, prospective buyers.

Once the demonstrations are over and I have greeted everyone, I take the event stage area where the red sparkly ribbon is ready for me to cut. While I'm delivering my speech, I suddenly feel uneasy. Now, I know there are a lot of eyes on me right now, but I feel as though I am being watched. My eyes flick to the back of the room, which is where the unnerving sensation is coming from. But there's nothing unordinary from what I can see, just the smiling faces of my guests.

When I'm finished, I speak to one of the guards. "Has everyone here definitely got an invitation?"

"Yes, Miss Alboni. Everyone has had their ticket scanned, identification checked, and bags searched on entry."

"And there's no way into this area without getting passed security?"

"No, Miss Alboni. Not a chance."

"Okay, thank you."

"Is everything okay?" The guard asks, concerned.

"Yes, fine, thank you." I don't bother saying anything else, as what am I supposed to tell him? It's probably nothing, but I just can't shake this feeling. And in the back of my mind, I know my intuition is always right.

Chapter 12

Mia

The launch continues with an afterparty at a bar we have hired. The venue has been beautifully dressed with the brand as its inspiration. There's been no expense spared with a free bar, food, and goody bags full of MIA cosmetics. Putting on my best show, I work my way around, networking. Everyone is enjoying themselves, and I have meetings with investors set up for the coming weeks. After a few hours, I am tired of business talk and go in search of my girls. I find Maria and Lucia at the bar, downing shots.

"Toilet break," they both insist as soon as they see me, then jump off their bar stools and take me by the arms into the ladies' room.

"So how is going? Have you been approached by any of the investors?" asks Marisa.

"Yes, a few actually."

"That's amazing. We're so proud of you, Mia." Lucia beams, and I know she means every word. As much as Lucia and Marisa live for the benefits of being in my life, they do care a lot about me.

"Hey, Mia, I know it's your night, but any chance we can go somewhere else when this is all over? I really want to find a nice English gentleman, and all the men here are either gay or old." Marisa pleads, and I wish I could take them somewhere and show them all London has to offer.

"Yeah, I've had enough of it all now." I agree. "The only problem is the guards. They'll follow us everywhere and not let anyone get near to us. That's if they even let me go somewhere that hasn't been security checked already."

"Argh, they spoil all our fun." Lucia stamps her feet while reapplying her lipstick. "It's a shame neither one of them are hot, but they both look like gorillas."

"We could lose them," suggests Marisa.

"Not possible." I sigh. "You girls can go. I'll just go back to the hotel."

The bathroom door then opens, and three women about our age walk in.

"Oh, my goodness. Mia, you look absolutely amazing! I love your dress."

One of the girls flings her arms around me, giving me a hug. I'll never get used to the fact that because people know me from the fashion world, they think that they know me enough to touch me, when in fact I don't know them from Adam.

Sensing my uneasiness, she pulls back. "I'm sorry. My name is Alice, and this is Brooke." She points at her blonde friend. "And this quiet one is Arianna," she adds, gesturing to the only dark-haired one of the trio. "We work for *Beauty Brand* magazine, and we are doing a piece on your event."

"We are so grateful to be here. We love the goody bags. I've been trying out the products already, and this lip gloss is just divine," Brooke chirps in while applying more gloss to her lips in the mirror.

"It's lovely to meet you girls. I'm so pleased you are enjoying it," I reply.

"Wow, you speak really good English. Like, I can't even tell you are Italian," says Alice.

Marisa laughs. "Another one of Mia's many talents. Her being fluent in many languages and able to mimic accents has been very useful over the years."

I smile and shake my head at Marisa, remembering all the times I used said talents as a teenager.

We have a good chat with them, and they tell us about a new club they are going to after the launch party.

"I've got VIP passes. You should all come. Plus we are celebrating tonight." Alice puts her arm around Arianna and continues. "Arianna has finally left her controlling, psycho of a husband."

Arianna smiles, but it doesn't quite reach her eyes. She hasn't said a word since she entered the bathroom.

"Unfortunately, that won't be possible for me, but you girls go," I suggest to Marisa and Lucia.

"I've got an idea," Marisa excitedly announces.

"What?" Lucia demands. "Please let it be a good one."

"Yes, yes, this will definitely work." Marisa eyes up our three new friends with her hands on her hips.

"Well, go on, then," I insist.

"We swap clothes!" Marisa exclaims.

Shaking my head, I disagree. "Nope, never going to work."

"Sure it will." Lucia starts taking one of blonde girls' hair down. "See, if we put their hair down, Brooke and Alice can pass for us and Arianna for you."

"Oh my goodness, yes! Let's do it," Brooke agrees.

"Do we get to keep your clothes, though?" Alices asks hopefully.

Looking at the girls, there's no way the

guards will fall for it. Yes, the girls have a similar build to us, and their hair is a similar colour, but they look nothing like us. Arianna is very plain looking and much shorter than me.

"Have you always lived in the UK, Arianna?" I ask, her olive complexion and dark eyes reminding me of my own.

"Since I was very young. But my father was Italian, and my mother was English. I seem to have gotten all my father's genes."

"Da quale parte d'Italia veniva?" *What part of Italy was he from?* I ask, thinking this may be a sign and considering the crazy idea.

"I'm sorry, I don't speak Italian. My parents both died when I was a baby." Arianna smiles, but I can see the pain behind it.

I don't question her any further. I just put my arm around her, giving her a little squeeze while offering my condolences.

"Please, Mia, let's just try it," Marisa interrupts.

"What's the worst that could happen? Come on, let's give it a try," Lucia begs.

Thinking for a moment, I have a quick look outside the bathroom to see where the guards are. One is stood at the front entrance and one at the back. We can't walk past them, as they'll see us. I think of a plan to get them to move away from the doors.

"Okay, let's do it. But we need to hurry up. We've been in here a while now, and the guards will be getting suspicious." I can't believe I am agreeing to this.

"You go back into the event, Mia, and make sure the guards see you. Get yourself a drink, then come back. Buy us some time while we make the girls look more like us," Lucia instructs excitedly.

"I've got my cordless straighteners in my bag, so I can do their hair," Marisa states while Lucia ushers me out of the door.

I make my way around the room, and speak to guests situated in front of the guards. I then go to the bar and ask for a glass of water. I sense one of the guards approach me from behind.

"Is everything okay, Miss Alboni?"

"Marisa drank a little too much. She is in the bathroom. I'm just getting her some water."

"Would you like me to arrange a car for her back to the hotel?"

"No, thank you. I'm sure she will be fine. You can arrange for the car to pick us up in one hour. I will be ready to go then. And stay by the door, please. I don't want any drunk idiots trying to get in." I point to the door where a group of men stand arguing with the bouncers.

"Yes, Miss Alboni." He then returns to the

door, and I go back to the bathroom.

Chapter 13

Mia

Suddenly I feel guilty. Marco is going to hit the roof when he finds out the guards lost us. I start to have doubts that this is even going to work until I walk into the bathroom. The girls have done an amazing job. Brooke and Alice now have their hair curled similar to Marisa and Lucia's, and Arianna's has been straightened to look more like mine. I'm impressed. All that's left to do now is swap clothes and accessories.

Once we are changed, I look at us through the mirror. Marisa, and Lucia, and I tie our hair up. I'm wearing Arianna's plain black dress that actually looks pretty good on me, considering it was bought from a high street chain.

"Okay, you three go into that cubical and lock the door. When the guards come in, stay nothing so they don't hear your voices and realise it's not us until they break down the door. Just bang on it so they know you're in there." Luckily the doors are floor to ceiling, so they can't look over. "We will go back in one by one. I'll go in last, then call the guards and tell them we are locked in the cubical. When they come to the bathroom, we will make a run for it. Just tell the guards we paid you to do it, and you have no idea where we have gone." I hand the girls a wad of £50 notes to make it believable. "Give it half an hour before you join us at the club, and make sure you're not followed."

The girls do as I instruct, and I enter the party unnoticed. I keep my head down and make the call to the guards. When I see them both go to the ladies' bathroom, I make a dash for the front exit, where I'm joined by my girls. We casually exit before making a run for it down a back street. Once we are far enough away, we all laugh and hug in excitement.

"I can't believe we did it!" exclaims Marisa.

"I know. But we need to get moving, as it won't be long until they realise. Do either of you know where we are going?"

"I've got the tickets here. I'll put the address in Google maps."

Seeing Lucia's phone makes me realise. "Shit. I'll have to get rid of my phone." Knowing Marco, he will have put a tracker on it.

"It's fine, we've got our phones. You can use them if needed," offers Marisa.

After logging out of my iCloud, I dump my phone in a bin.

"It's a left down here." Lucia leads the way.

We are walking down a main road, and I sense a car driving slowly behind us. There's no traffic, and I notice that the road is closed to drivers at this time in the evening, leaving it free for pedestrians. I continue talking to the girls so not to alarm them and take out my compact mirror to check behind me. Seeing the black vehicle curb crawling behind us, I know we are in trouble. It's not one of our cars. Dread fills me.

Noticing a narrow alleyway to our left, I grab both girls and pull them in. "This way, girls—quick."

"But the map says it's to the right," Lucia disagrees and holds up her phone.

Hearing the doors of the car open, my worst fears are confirmed.

"Take your shoes off and run," I instruct.

"Bloody hell, how did they find us so quick?"

"That's not the guards, Marisa. Come on, run." Holding their hands, I run with all my might. The girls struggle to keep up with me, but I keep going.

I can hear heavy, fast-paced footsteps behind us.

Then I hear a sharp, sudden blast.

They've got a silencer on the gun, but I

know a gunshot when I hear one. Marsia drops to the ground. Screams of pain echo through the alleyway. She holds her leg in agony.

"Get her up!" I scream at Lucia. We put Marisa's arms over our shoulders and struggle to keep moving.

"Stop…. I can't!" Marisa cries.

"Please, Marisa, we need to keep going," I implore. "Focus on running. Come on, we need to keep going."

They're gaining on us. Ahead, I see lights—the opening of the next street. If we can just make it to the open road, we can find safety. But it feels like the alleyway never ends. Our legs are moving, but we don't cover much distance.

Another sharp blast sounds, followed by a piercing scream from Lucia.

Lucia falls, and Marisa follows her, pulling me down as they go. The white material around Lucia's back is turning red. My heart races. I can hear my pulse in my ears. My girls cry in pain. I wrap my arms around them.

"I'm so sorry," I whisper.

Anger and adrenaline now fill my body. I get up and stand in between them and the shooter.

"ENOUGH!" Trying to shield them with my body, I plead, "Take me. That's what you've come for, isn't it? Leave them alone."

Two large men approach us in the shadows. Their faces are covered. One of them wraps this hand painfully around my upper arm, while the other slams the handle of this gun into my temple, my head knocked to one side with the force, almost breaking my neck. My legs give way as light-headedness washes over me. My knees hit the ground before I'm dragged along by my arm. The skin on my legs scrapes against the rough, wet pavement.

The sound of screams arouses me from my daze.

"No, please no!" I hear Lucia beg.

I turn to see the other man holding his gun towards my friends. Before I can react, he pulls the trigger. Lucia's body slumps lifelessly to the ground. The haunting scream of Marisa fills my ears. I push to my feet to get to them, fighting with all my might to get free from my captor. With an elbow to his face and groin, I get free, but it's too late. He fires a bullet into the back of Marisa's head.

I run towards them. When I reach my friends, I cradle them in my arms. Screams of heartache burst from my lungs. They're gone. My body shakes uncontrollably as I hold them. Guilt fills my chest. We should never have left the launch. This is all my fault; I brought these girls into my dangerous world.

Holding them tightly, I cry with sorrow,

apologising repeatedly. Abruptly I'm ripped from the embrace. Too heartbroken to fight back, I let them pull me away. My body convulses, and my stomach empties in front of me. I'm rewarded with a crack to the back of my head. But it doesn't hurt. I'm too numb. With a last look back at my friends as I reach the end of the alleyway, I silently promise my girls I will avenge their deaths. The car that was following us is parked on the road at the end of the alleyway. One of the men pushes me into the back seat, his gun pressed into the back of my head. The other gets into the seat in front of me and starts the engine.

"Who are you? What do you want from me?" Neither man has said a word to me, and both remain quiet. I do, however, notice the glances they keep giving each other.

As we set off, I assess my situation. The man beside me is still pointing his gun at me. The man in front has put his gun away in order to drive. Their first mistake was not restraining me. Amateurs. When the moment is right, I have no doubt I will kill them both. Their orders were obviously not to kill me, so I have that on my side. Plus, I have no care for my own life after the murder of my friends. My only motivation now is to end theirs.

A phone vibrates in the man's pocket at my side. As he reaches to get it, the hand holding the gun naturally relaxes. Here's my chance. With my right hand, I grab the gun while forcing my left elbow into his neck and crushing his windpipe. Stunned, he gasps for breath but unfortunately doesn't loosen his grip on his gun. Struggling with all my might, I try to release his hand, but he overpowers me, headbutting me in the temple.

My adrenaline allows me to fight on, and the trigger is pulled. A shot is fired.

It's not me who is hit.

We are suddenly thrown back into our seats as the car accelerates forward. The driver is slumped over the steering wheel.

Continuing to wrestle with the man beside me, I manage to turn the gun towards him. My finger finds the trigger. I press over and over. His eyes bulge as he fights for his life. Eventually he stops fighting, and his body stills. His eyes glaze over as life leaves him. Releasing the gun from his hand, I fire one final shot between his eyes. That one's for my girls.

The car then throws me to the side, my head banging into the side window as we mount the pavement. I dive into the front of the car, and I try to take control of the steering wheel under the driver's dead weight. When I pull the wheel as much as I can, the car moves a little towards the road, but it's not enough.

In front of us, I see the girls dressed in our clothes run out of the bar, the guards following after them. There's nothing I can do to stop the car driving into them at speed. I shout and scream for them to move, but they don't hear me. I frantically search for the horn on the car to alert them. But it is too late. Their bodies hit the bonnet, then the windscreen at full force. Arianna's head penetrates and showers me with glass. The car continues and moves back onto the road. Out of nowhere, another car appears. I have no way to stop myself from driving straight into it at full speed.

The collision throws me from the car. I am powerless to stop myself moving. I'm tossed around like a rag doll. I feel bones crack and my skin split. Pain rushes through me. Everything seems to be happening in slow motion. I feel stabs of agony with each impact I endure. Eventually my body feels heavy, and I realise I am still. Adrenaline fills me. Fighting for my life, I try to get up, but I can't. I have no control. I'm paralysed. It's eerily silent.

I make peace with the fact that this is my end. But before I can drift off into that never-ending sleep, an almighty bang ripples through my every nerve. I feel light again. But that is when I feel the heat. The scorching and melting sensation on my skin. I smell burning flesh. I smell death.

Chapter 14

Marco

"Why are they not answering my calls!" I boom.

"I've got a team that should be there any minute now," Van replies as his phone rings. He looks at the caller ID and nods at me. It's them.

"Well?" Van listens intently.

Watching him, I know there is a problem. He rubs his forehead with his hand.

"What? What the fuck is going on?" I demand.

Van holds his hand up to stop me. "And Mia?" he shouts down the phone. His head then slumps. Ending the call, he turns to me. Emotion fills his face.

Pain in my gut almost cripples me. "Tell me!" I bellow.

"There's been an incident. The team are trying to find out what exactly happened. There has been an explosion outside the bar where the launch event was being held. A car mounted the pavement, then drove headfirst into another car. Mia and the girls were in the middle of it."

"What do you mean, they were in the middle of it?" This doesn't make sense.

"They are getting the CCTV footage and sending it over to us as soon as they have it."

"Organise the jet. We are going to England."

It's the longest plane ride ever. I cannot sit down. I am pacing up and down the plane, feeling helpless.

"Sit the fuck down!" Mia and Van's father rages at me.

Before I can even think about it, my hands are around his neck, and I'm dragging him out of his chair. Mia's father, Mr. Alboni, used to be the underboss of the Guerra a generation ago, but he's just an old man now, and I've never liked him. Van intervenes before I do permanent damage.

"This isn't helping." Vans separates us as his phone pings with an alert. "The CCTV has come through."

He shares the grainy video to the plane's television. Their surveillance should have been updated before the event. We all watch in silence as the screen fills with the inside of the bar. It starts with Mia and her two friends Lucia and

Marisa quickly exiting the ladies' bathroom. The guards then appear, chasing after them. The girls run outside, and the guards follow quickly behind them. The video then switches to the cameras at the front of the building. The guards are shouting at the girls on the pavement.

They don't even notice the car speeding up the pavement until it's too late. The car hits all five of them at force. Their bodies bounce off the car, then fly through the air, apart from Mia, who impales the windscreen. But the car does not stop. Another car appears, driving in the opposite direction. They collide headfirst at speed. The first car mounts the second and flips backwards, landing on its roof. Seconds later the car on its roof explodes. The car containing Mia, my Mia. The cameras go dead, and the screen fills with darkness.

The plane is eerily silent as we all stare at the black screen, unable to believe what we just witnessed. Standing up, I turn and rip the chair I was sitting on from the bolts on the floor. I throw it down the aisle of the plane. The feeling inside of me is unbearable. I want to rip out my heart. The television takes the hit next when I pull it from it brackets and smash it onto the floor. Moving down the plane, I connect my fists with the walls and then the plane door. Alarms sound as I continue to beat the metal handle on the plane door.

"Enough!" Van bellows.

And I stop, taking a deep breath to expand my collapsing lungs.

He puts his hands on my shoulders. "That is my sister I have just watched being blown to smithereens!" he barks, emotion cracking his voice. Bowing his head, he takes a breath before looking me in the eyes again. "You are my boss. The leader of the Guerra. Now get your fucking act together and lead."

I don't reply. I can't. I just pant, trying to catch my breath.

Leaving me to my thoughts, he goes and sits with his father. Van is right. It shouldn't be him taking control of the situation—it should be me. Pushing my feelings down, I stand tall and return to Van and the others.

"I need to know who was driving those cars. And why the girls were trying to get away from the guards."

The team on the plane get to work. With my mind occupied, we soon arrive in London.

When we arrive at the bar, the street has already been cleared. The cars are gone, and the road is being sprayed down. The water runs red down the street, flowing into the nearest drain. Police have the area cordoned off.

"I will speak to the police. We don't have the MPS on our payroll. You will end up getting arrested," Van advises, then he and his father go in search of who is in charge while I take in the scene.

The front windows of the bar have been boarded up. The sign above them is broken and melted. The walls above are covered in the black remnants of smoke. So many questions bounce around my mind. This wasn't an accident, but this also wasn't an assassination. Why didn't they just shoot them? I need to see Mia. I cannot believe she is dead.

"We are going to the police station," Van informs me when he returns with his father.

"I'll come with you," I insist.

"No. It is next of kin and family only," Mr. Alboni replies.

"I said I'll come with you!" I swear on my life, one day I will kill this man. Nobody tells me what to do.

Chapter 15

Marco

At the police station, Mr. Alboni and Van go into a meeting room. I'm instructed to wait outside. I'm furious, but I need to keep calm. We have no jurisdiction in this country. However, I manage to speak to one of the officers who have been at the scene, and thankfully he is helpful. I find out where the cars have been taken, and I send one of my teams to go and gather some evidence of our own. I need to find out who was in those cars.

"I need DNA samples from both vehicles." I end the call to my forensic team as Van returns.

Van speaks more quietly than I've ever heard him. "She's gone, Marco."

"I want to see her," I insist.

"Unfortunately, that won't be possible," an officer calls from behind him.

"Come on." Van puts his hand on my back and leads me outside towards the car. I cannot comprehend what I have just been told. Van continues, "My father's staying to sign some forms. Mia's body was unrecognisable when they extinguished the car. They're taking some DNA to match what they found. Once they have a result, we will have Mia's remains sent home." Van doesn't look at me when he talks. "I know you and Mia were close, Marco. But I need you to get it together and find the fuckers who did this."

My body erupts into an almighty growl. I can't control my emotions. I want to hammer my head into a wall until I forget. Van backs away from me while I take my frustration out on a nearby fence, kicking and punching the wooden panel until it resembles nothing but firewood. After releasing some anger, I turn to see Van, along with a few police officers, stood watching me. The police look relieved to see I've calmed down and there's no need for them to intervene. When we get into our waiting car, neither I nor Van speak. I feel my heart harden more than it ever has been before. My eyes glaze. It's like I'm wearing tinted glasses—everything I see is red. My whole future has been stolen from me. All I see now is death. My life now will consist of finding those responsible, inflicting horrendous pain, and slowly sending them to their deaths.

We spend a few days in London, watching video after video from surrounding surveillance cameras. But we come up with nothing. The first car comes at speed from much further down the road before the girls even make their way out of the bar. I have no doubt Mia was a target, but it does seem like that the car incident was the original plan. What *was* the original plan, however, we still have no idea. The guards are both deceased, and witnesses give no other explanation. One of the drivers from the second car got away. I have issued a million-euro reward to anyone who can bring him to me alive, so it's only a matter of time.

When Mia's father receives the DNA results from the car, it is confirmed as a positive match for Mia. The little hope I had for a miracle dies, so we return home.

During our time in England, Lorenzo's forty-eight hours came to an end. Although he dropped all charges, he is still making things very difficult for us. After we released all the hostages unharmed, rumours started to spread amongst civilians that we had tortured the law enforcement. Organisations who have been allies for generations have cut ties with us, making deliveries and distribution of weapons more difficult. The Martelé, our archenemies, have also reared their ugly heads, starting to fight for our territories. Lorenzo has resigned and gone into hiding, but I will find him. I haven't finished with that weasel yet.

As I sit at my desk, my thoughts are filled with Mia. The way she made me feel when I was around her—the way only she could make me feel: like I was human. A feeling I haven't felt since she passed. My thoughts, as always, turn from happiness to immense anger and pain when I remember she has been taken away from me. I down the last of my scotch and throw my glass against the door, narrowly missing Van as he enters.

"Sober up. We have found the guy from the second car. He is being flown over as we speak."

Finally. It's been two weeks since Mia died. I am ready to inflict some pain.

Everything is set up in the basement when Van enters, dragging a terrified looking man along with him. Van throws him onto the floor in front of me. I don't speak. I just watch as he takes in the room around him through his swollen, beaten eyes, whimpering as he sees the tools ready to inflict pain and end his life. His focus then lands on me and my bloodstained apron.

"Tie him to the chair."

My men instantly do as I ask, fastening his arms and legs to the wooden chair.

"Two weeks ago, a Guerra woman, my woman, was murdered. You were in one of the cars responsible for her death."

The man looks at the floor, not acknowledging me.

"Look at me!" My right fist connects with his jaw. His head jerks backwards cracking into the back of the chair. "Tell me your assignment for that night!"

The man is a little dazed from my attack but manages to mumble, "I… cant. They will kill me."

A bark of a laugh rips through me. "And what do you think I'm going to do with you? Wrap you up in bandages and let you go? Let me explain what is going to happen. Today is the day that you will die. What time this happens and how painful your death is up to you." I pace the room around him while I speak, noticing the gurgling sound from his chest as he breathes, a sign blood is filling his lungs, a result of the beats he's received in transit. Unfortunately that means we don't have as long as I'd hoped.

After selecting my first choice of torturing device, I stand over the man. He takes one look at what I am holding and pisses himself. I turn on the blowtorch and slowly move it towards his hand.

"Okay! Okay! Please. I'll tell you all I know."

I keep on holding the flame near his hand, and he continues quickly while trying to move from the heat.

"I'm just a driver. Just to and from places, usually. I've never been involved in any of their missions before. I was told to park up and wait. Then when the target was in sight, the soldiers in the back would get out, grab her, and put her in the car. Then I would drive to the location given."

"Soldiers?" I ask.

"Yeah, that's what they call them."

"What who calls them?" I move the flame of the torch directly onto his hand, melting the skin until blood and tissue appear. He screams in agony until I stop.

"Carry on. Who were you working for?" I demand.

Crying in pain, he explains. "I never met them directly. I owed some money, a lot of money. I was told if I did this job, my debt would be wiped clean."

"I don't care for excuses. Give me a fucking name!" I move the flame to his other hand, holding it there for a few seconds before removing it. Once his screams subside, I ask again. "The name of who you were working for?"

"Mart... something. Mattel, maybe? Th-they never directly t-told me," he stutters.

I watch him, reading him. He's telling the truth.

"The Martelé?" I prompt.

"Yes. That's it. They were foreign. Had an accent like you," he confirms.

"Tell me what happened." I put down the

torch, encouraging him to speak.

"We were stationed down the road from the bar. There was another car on the next street who were given the same instructions. They were watching the back exit. We watched for hours, waiting for them to leave. One of the soldiers then spotted the targets leaving, they told me to drive towards them, so I did. The next minute the other car came speeding towards us. I thought it was going to stop, but it didn't—it just kept coming and coming. It went straight into those people and then into us."

I push for more. "Why do you think the plan changed?"

"I have no idea. One of the soldiers received a call a few minutes before it all happened. I don't know what was said, as I didn't understand their language. I was just told to wait. Then the other car came flying towards us. It was out of control, like the driver didn't know where they were going."

The pain in my chest throbs as I relive watching the video of Mia being stuck, her helpless body burning in flames. I retrieve the blowtorch and turn it on full, I set the man's arm alight. His howls of suffering don't come close to the pain I feel inside.

I drop the torch to the floor, then remove my apron. "You finish him off," I instruct one on my men. "Find out every detail, who contacted him, times, dates, descriptions."

When I leave the basement, Van follows me upstairs.

"What the hell was that?" he asks, annoyed.

"He doesn't know anything else of importance. I need to kill the Martelé."

"Marco, you can't kill all the Martelé. They just declared war, yes. But we need to find out more. Going after them now will just be a blood bath for us all."

"What more is there to find out? They killed Mia, your sister!" I argue, frustrated that he doesn't also want to rip their heads off immediately.

"Believe me, there's nothing I want more than to end each and every one of their miserable lives, but there's more to this. He said they were there to kidnap her, not kill her."

"What's the fucking difference. They did kill her," I reply getting more and more irritated.

"But why? Why did the plan change?"

"Who the fuck knows. All I know is, the Martelé are responsible for her death, and I will bring the whole organisation to its knees if it's the last thing I do!"

Walking away from protesting Van, I return to my office and go over my revenge. Tonight the Martelé will pay. It's not the first time I have killed their leader. Three years ago, I killed Antonio Martelé to save my boss and his wife. There's been conflict between the Guerras and their organisation throughout the generations, for one reason or another. When Leonardo Guerra, the last boss of the Guerras, and his wife died, the hostility of the Martelé leader's murder died with them. Or so we thought. We knew there would always be bad blood between us, but I'd assumed assassinations of the Guerra were off the cards. I should have known better. I took my eyes off them, and as a result, my Mia paid the ultimate price.

Chapter 16

Mia

So, this is what death feels like. Nothing. I can't move or open my eyes. I'm just floating around in darkness. Well, this is unexpected. Not that I had thought much about what happens after I die, but I either though it would be completely nothing, where I couldn't hear myself think, or there would be something—anything. Other people who had also passed, maybe. I'd considered that I might end up in hell, given all the terror I had been involved with in my life. Maybe this is hell. A life of loneliness. At least it is peaceful.

I can't hear anything other than the voice in my head. No, wait, I do hear something. Is that someone talking? It's muffled. No, it's gone.

There it is again. It is definitely a voice. I can't quite make out what it's saying, though.

I'm feeling different now. I can feel, which is different. Everything is heavy, and I can feel my arms. I can't move them, but I definitely feel them now.

I'm starting to feel my body. Maybe I'm not dead. Maybe I'm asleep.

Yes, it's definitely voices I can hear.

"Arianna? I think she's waking up."

Arianna—do I recognise that name? My eyes feel lighter. I can open them. It's blurry, but I can see the silhouettes of two people. Panic sets in as I try to talk, but I choke. There's something in my throat. Gasping for breath, I try and lift my arms to remove what is restricting me. But my arms won't move.

"Just relax, Arianna. You are safe in hospital. There is a tube in your mouth to help you breathe. I'm going to give you something to relax you. When you wake again, you will feel much better."

A second later I am back in the darkness.

When I wake again, I'm not sure I would say I feel better. I'm no longer choking, which I am thankful for, but my throat is excruciating. Swallowing is difficult, and my mouth is dry and sore. My eyes roam the area around me. I'm in a small room, lying in a bed.

There is a man sitting at my side. As I turn to look at him, I feel the pressure of something covering my face. This time I manage to lift one of my arms up in front of me. Bandages weigh heavy, covering my hand to my elbow. Someone else enters the room. A doctor I presume from the way he is dressed.

"Arianna, it is good to see you awake. I'm Doctor Clarke. I'm one of your consultants. Would it be okay if we had a little chat?" He pulls a seat up to the side of my bed. "Firstly, I just want to make you aware that you are in the hospital, we are taking very good care of you, and you are doing remarkably well. Your husband is here, and you have no need to worry." The doctor gestures to the man sitting at the other side of my bed.

I have no recollection of this man whatsoever. When I try and speak, no words come out. All I can do is cough. The pain I feel throughout my body when my chest heaves for air is crippling.

"Arianna, please relax and don't try and talk just yet. I'm going to hold your hand, and I want you to squeeze it once for yes and twice for no." The doctor takes my hand gently in his. "Do you understand?"

I squeeze his hand.

"Yes, good job, Arianna. Two weeks ago, you were involved in a very serious accident. Do you remember the accident?"

I think for a moment. Nothing. I know I should remember; I know I have memories. It's like they are in a locked cabinet, and I just can't turn the key far enough to release them. I squeeze his hand twice.

"No. That's perfectly understandable, Arianna. You have suffered a serious head injury, and it will take time to recover. But I assure you, I will do everything I can to help you get back to yourself."

My breath catches, and an emotional cry releases from my lips.

"During the accident, you sustained many bone fractures and second and third degree burns to your face, chest, and limbs. When you were brought into the hospital, we felt it was best to place you in an induced coma in order to let your brain get the rest it needed and have the greatest chance of recovery. During the past few weeks, we have performed multiple skin graft procedures, which involved shaving a thin layer of healthy skin and covering the damaged areas with it. I'm pleased to say these operations were very successful, and we expect minimal scarring. But Arianna, you have a long road of recovery ahead of you."

The doctor continues to talk, but my mind is elsewhere. It's too much to comprehend. I'm frustrated I can't remember anything. I feel trapped in my own body. I want to rip myself out of my skin and run free. But I can't.

"I'm going to leave you now to get some rest, as you've had a lot to take in."

The doctor lets go of my hand and asks the

man who I'm told is my husband to join him outside the room.

As they leave, a nurse enters.

"Arianna, it's lovely to see you awake. My name is Donna. I'm one of your nurses." She takes hold of my hand. Her hand is warm, and her eyes are comforting. "Now, are you in any pain, Arianna? Squeeze once for yes, twice for no."

I squeeze her hand. I'm so uncomfortable.

"I thought so. Right, I'm going to give you some pain relief through your IV. Then in about ten minutes, once the medication has started to work, I'm going to change your dressings. Is that ok with you?"

I squeeze her hand.

Donna is one of those people you can't help but like. She has a beautiful smile and is kind and caring. When she removes the dressings and cleans my wounds, she is gentle and constantly checks how I am feeling. She assures me I won't be left with too much scarring and that the surgeons have done an incredible job.

"You are so beautiful, Arianna," Donna compliments as she treats the skin on my face. "How about a drink of water? Would you like to try having a drink?"

As soon as she takes hold of my hand for me to answer, I squeeze it tightly. My mouth is dry as a bone.

Donna giggles at my response. "I take it that's a yes. I will be right back."

Donna leaves the room, and the man who is my husband returns. He walks over to my bedside and takes hold of my hand. His face is full of concern.

"Do you know who I am?" he asks.

I squeeze his hand twice.

"Do you remember anything from your life before your accident?"

I squeeze his hand twice again.

He remains silent for a moment, staring at my face. "I am your husband. My name is Eric. We love each other very much, and we are going to have a happy life together."

I feel as though he is talking to himself as much as to me. I suppose this must be very hard on him too. The fact that I can't remember who he is must break his heart. Eric is of a medium build. He has green eyes and reddish-brown hair. I wouldn't say he is an attractive man, more average. When I look at him, I feel no comfort. I know I don't remember him, but even looking at my nurse Donna, I felt something. With him, I feel nothing.

Donna returns with a jug of water and glass.

"Ahh, you must be so relieved to see her

awake, Eric!" Donna beams as she looks between us.

Eric drops my hand and sits beside me. "She doesn't know who I am," he explains.

"Oh, don't worry. I'm sure Arianna will remember you soon. Why don't you bring some photographs of the two of you on your wedding day or holidays. It may help jog her memory," Donna suggests while raising my bed so I'm in a more upright position.

"I don't think that's a good idea. It might upset her," Eric disagrees.

"Whatever you think, Eric. You know Arianna best. Now let's get some water in you."

Donna puts the glass of water to my lips, and I gulp it down in one. It's the most delicious water I have ever tasted.

"Well done, Arianna. Maybe later we will try something to eat, then we can take that feeding tube out of your nose, which will make you more comfortable. Now you get some rest." Donna lays me back down and dims the lights a little.

I do feel exhausted, and it's not long before I'm fast asleep.

My mind unfortunately doesn't rest. I have nightmare after nightmare. *It's dark. I'm running away from something terrifying. The sound of harrowing screams fills my ears. I feel burning pain.*

Thick smoke fills my lungs, and I'm choaking.

I wake, gasping for air. There's a lady stood beside my bed, petting my hand.

"It's okay, it's okay." She smiles sympathetically. "Just a dream."

The small grey-haired lady puts me at ease, and I relax a little.

"I'm Elena. I'm your nurse in the evening. I get the pleasure of the night shift." She chuckles sweetly to herself. "I've been waiting to see those big brown eyes for weeks. They are just as lovely as I expected. So beautiful. Such shiny dark hair and olive skin. Unusual for an English girl. You remind me of my daughter." Elena speaks with an accent.

"Her dad was Italian," Eric chips in from the corner of the room.

I hadn't realised he was there.

"Ahh, meravigliosa, meravigliosa!" *Wonderful, wonderful!* Elena claps her hands excitedly. "Da dove vieni in Italia?" *Where in Italy are you from?*

"She doesn't speak Italian," Eric interrupts.

I reply, "Mi dispiace di non ricordare." *I'm sorry, I don't remember.* I'm surprised by my sudden ability to talk, albeit with only a croak of a voice.

"I meant she doesn't *like* to speak Italian. Please speak to her in English," Eric says when he gets a funny look from Elena.

"Okay, please forgive me." She frowns, seeming displeased by Eric. "I'm also Italian. Such a beautiful country. I moved here with my family twenty years ago—" Elena is interrupted by Eric grunting in the corner. Clearly sensing his frustration, she changes the subject. "Right then, Arianna, let's get you another drink, and then we will get you something to eat."

After taking a drink, I'm feeling more awake and a little hungry.

"Now, on your notes, it's doesn't say anything about any allergies. Are there definitely no intolerances I need to be aware of, Eric?" Elena asks.

Eric shakes his head.

"Good. How about a yogurt to start off with, Arianna?"

"Yes, please," I whisper trying to gain control over my voice.

Eric eventually leaves to go home and rest, which I am thankful for. I know he cares about me, but I feel uncomfortable with him sat staring at me all day. Elena takes good care of me through the night. I'm given some more pain relief, and thankfully I have a good sleep without being interrupted by nightmares. In the morning the doctor comes to see me.

"Good morning, Arianna, Eric. I've come to discuss a few things with you." The doctor takes a seat beside me, and Eric does the same. "Now when you came into hospital, we did some blood tests, something we do with all our patients being admitted. We test for things like blood type, as we didn't have yours on record, antibodies, infection levels, things like that. However, one thing that came up in your bloods, your husband wasn't aware of," the doctor explains, and his voice slows, making me worry. "You are in fact pregnant, Arianna."

The information hits me like a ton of bricks. How can this be happening to me? I look at Eric, who seems quite happy with the revelation.

"Your HCG levels are high and have stayed so, indicating you are around eight to twelve weeks. We will be able to confirm that with an ultrasound. But..."

I don't like the sound of that "but". I can't say I'm happy with any of this—however, I couldn't face something else being wrong.

"During your accident you sustained a number of extensive injuries that could have impacted the pregnancy. We then have given you multiple medications, and you've been through many medical procedures, which again could have affected the baby. Your bloods do give us some hope, but I need you to keep an open mind,

Arianna, and you, too, Eric. We need to take each day as it comes."

Wow, I can't even put into words how I feel. I'm stunned into silence, so frustrated this is even my life. I feel like I'm trapped.

The doctor makes arrangements for me to have a scan this morning. I'm pleased I don't have to wait long. The porters arrive to take me to the maternity unit to have a scan. The nurses unclip my IV medication and fluids and attach them to the bed for transportation. The porters release the brakes on my bed and wheel me down the bright corridors. The florescent ceiling lights have me closing my eyes. It takes about five minutes to reach the unit after a lift ride and many swinging doors. I'm taken into a dark room, which pleases my eyes. Around me are ultrasound machines with screens and coloured flashing lights. Eric appears and stands at my side, looking concerned.

Eric tries to comfort me. "Don't worry, it will be okay."

But it has no effect. To be honest, I'm not really feeling anything emotionally. Just pain from my injuries and frustration at my lack of control.

"Hello, Arianna, I'm Sally, and I'm going to be performing your ultrasound today."

"Hello, Sally," I say, my voice becoming much clearer.

Sally sits beside me on a high stool and pulls a machine along with her. "I just need to raise your gown so I can get to your abdomen." Sally pulls my bed sheet down to my hips and lifts my gown, exposing my stomach, which still has visible bruising. "I'll be gentle." She smiles sympathetically.

After rubbing gel onto my stomach, she places the scanner on my skin. Slowly and gently, she moves it from side to side. Lying there staring at the ceiling, I try again to remember something. Anything will do. A tiny memory about my life before the accident. But nothing. Why can't I remember?

"Just try to relax." Sally speaks to me softly, clearly noticing me tensing my body. "I've almost finished with my checks, then I'll turn the screen and show you your baby."

My what now? I know that's what I'm having the scan for, but it really hadn't registered. Although I hoped nothing would be wrong, I hadn't thought about what that actually meant. For nothing else to be wrong, it means I am having a baby—me. Who is *me*? How can I look after a baby when I can't even remember who I am.

"Here we are," Sally says as she turns the screen towards me and Eric. "Baby is measuring about ten weeks. Everything looks perfectly normal for this stage. You both must be so relieved." Sally beams at us.

I look at Eric, who has a smile that reaches both ears. He's nodding in agreement.

"Yes, so relieved," Eric replies, then asks Sally questions, like when will know if it's a boy or a girl, can she tell if it's been hurt during my accident, and so on.

But I switch off. I can't even think about a baby right now.

Chapter 17

Mia

With each week that passes, I get a little bit stronger. I've started to walk with the help of physiotherapists and a lot of determination on my part. My bones are fully healed now thanks to the operations I had while in a coma and the bed rest I have had for the last six weeks. Unfortunately, having hardly moved for those weeks, my muscles have pretty much disintegrated. I'm now trying to build them up. I need to be careful with my skin, as it's still healing from the burns, so I can't overdo it, but the sooner I can walk, the sooner I'll feel more myself, I'm sure.

My memory still hasn't returned. The doctors aren't sure it ever will. But I'm not giving up hope. Unlike my husband Eric, who seems unbothered by the fact I have no memory of our wedding and life together before the accident. He just keeps saying we are going to make new memories. Which is fine, as I know he's trying to cheer me up. However, I'm not giving up.

"So tell me about our school. What did it

look like? Where was it?" I ask Eric. Everyday while eating our lunch he tells me about our past, hoping it will jog my memory.

"We went to St. Mary's. That's where we met. It's a big school, primary and secondary. In primary school we didn't really know each other. It was secondary when we were made lab partners in science," Eric explains while eating his sandwich with his mouth open, and bits of egg mayo shoot from his mouth as he speaks.

I'm trying so hard, but I just can't see what I ever saw in him.

"It was love at sight for both of us."

That has me barking a laugh, much to Eric's annoyance. But I mean, come on. I've looked at myself in the mirror, and even with these scars, which are thankfully fading now, I am so far out of his league.

Trying to defend himself, he adds, "You had a mouth full of braces and a face full of acne, but I loved you anyway."

I roll my eyes at his comment and continue questioning him. "And what about my friends? I know I had two who died in the accident, but I must have had more. Am I still in touch with any of them?" I continue hoping someone else might be able to help me.

"No. You don't keep in contact with anyone

from school."

"Let me get this straight. I don't have any friends from school, and I haven't worked since I left school. My parents died when I was a baby, and I was brought up in care, where I had a terrible time. I have no other relatives?"

"Yes, that's right," Eric confirms, spitting a piece of egg across the room.

"Do you think the family of my friends—what were their names again? Alice and Brooke? Do you think they might speak to me?"

"No, not for a while, anyway. It's too soon, what with you surviving and them not," Eric explains.

I suppose that is understandable.

"So all I have is you?"

"Yes, it's all we've ever needed. Each other." He smiles, showing his teeth, which have food all stuck in between them.

I'm just not buying it. I can't for a minute believe I would have a life that only consisted of him. I can't wait to get out into the world to be free. I feel trapped in here, only seeing the same faces. Surely I must have felt like that before my accident. Unless the event has completely changed my mindset.

"Arianna, Eric, great—I'm glad you're both here. I have some good news." my doctor announces while tapping the file in his hand.

"Brillant. I could do with some good news, Doc," I confess.

"I've been speaking to your physios, and they are really impressed with your progress. I think we can start arranging for you to go home."

"Excellent news," I agree.

"There are some things we need to arrange to ensure that you will be safe and comfortable at home, but that will only take a week or so. And you need to be able to walk up and down steps safely, which the physios assure me you'll be able to do any day now. If we aim for a week's time, will that be okay for you both?"

"That's good for me. Is that okay for you, Eric?" I ask, trying to read his expression.

"Yes, wonderful. I can't believe I actually get to take you home," Eric says enthusiastically, as if he can't believe his luck.

"Ahh, yes, Eric, it's been a very worrying time for you both," the doctor sympathises. "Any development with your memory, Arianna? Has looking at photographs helped at all?"

I look at Eric in annoyance. Every day, he has had an excuse as to why he hasn't brought any. "I still haven't seen any." I glare at Eric.

"Like I keep telling Arianna, we were in the process of moving when she had her accident, and all our belonging were in storage, so I haven't been able to get hold of them."

The doctor looks at Eric in confusion. Then he opens his file and turns a few pages. "So you no longer live at this address?" The doctor shows the file to Eric.

"No, we've moved. Well, I've moved us."

"Ahh, that's a shame. I was hoping when Arianna returned home, she would recognise it. Never mind. Having all her things around her should have the same effect. Let's get your new address down, and then we can start arranging for Arianna to go home. Do you not have any photos on your phone, Eric?"

"You'd think that, wouldn't you," I reply for Eric. "Only Eric has a brick of a phone from the medieval era, by the looks of it. It doesn't even have a colour screen."

"How unfortunate," says the doctor. "I'm sure once you're home things will come back to you."

Eric follows the doctor out of the room, leaving me with Donna, who I've become quite close with.

"So how do you feel about going home?" Donna asks, seeming concerned.

"I'm definitely ready to get out of hospital, I'm not sure how I feel about living with Eric. I've tried to see what I must have seen before, but I just can't," I admit.

Donna nods in agreement, clearly not surprised by my confession. "I think the best thing you can do is concentrate on getting yourself better and that baby of yours. I'm sure in time, everything will sort itself out one way or another."

Sitting on my bed deep in thought, I eat the chocolate bar Eric brought me as part of my lunch. The hospital food is okay, but after this many weeks, I've had enough. The chocolate bar is a Snickers. Eric said it was my favourite. I have to admit, it is pretty amazing. It's funny, though—I don't recognise the taste. Although my memory is completely gone, when I've eaten other food, I knew what they would taste like before I ate them. But with this, it's like a brand-new experience.

I read the wrapper as I devour the last piece. Nougat topped with caramel and peanuts, all encased in milk chocolate. That was a good chocolate bar—my mouth is even tingling. While I'm thinking about finally leaving the hospital and what my future will hold, I start to feel strange. The tingling in my mouth has moved down to my throat.

Donna is at my side, sorting out my medication when she puts her hand on my arm. "Arianna, are you feeling okay? You look a little flushed." Donna retrieves her thermometer and places it in my ear.

When I go to answer, my breath is caught by a tightness in my throat, and I start to cough. "My throat... tight." I sit up in panic as I struggle for each breath.

"Don't panic. I'm going to get you some help." Donna presses a button at the side of my bed, and a high pitch alarm sounds immediately.

A doctor and two nurses rush into my room.

"I think she's going into anaphylactic shock," Donna informs them.

"We need adrenaline now," the doctor instructs one of the nurses, who quickly exits the room. "Get her lying down."

Donna gently pushes me back and drops my bed into a lying position. "It's going to be okay, Arianna. Just lie back and try to relax."

I try to answer, but my tongue is swollen and won't let me respond. My chest is now convulsing as it fights for oxygen. The room around me starts to spin. My eyes fill with bright twinkling lights. I hear the nurse return, and the four of them speak quickly and loudly to each other, but I am unable to make out what they're saying. It's like my head is under water. Everything is muffled and there is a strange echoing sound. They must administer some sort of medication, as I feel my body start to rest slightly. My eyes close of their own accord, and

I drift into darkness.

Chapter 18

Marco

"Boss, they're here!" Van booms behind me.

But I don't move. I need another minute with Mia. I'm stood by her gravestone, reading the engraved words over and over like I have done every day since we buried her ashes in my garden. "Much loved daughter and sister."

But that's not all she was. She was loved by me. I loved her.

However, I never got to tell her what she meant to me. The Martelé took her away from me before I had the chance. The focus of my existence since she left has been to end everyone who had a hand in her murder. But I have failed her again. Now the Martelé have the house surrounded. The fight in me has run out. At least I will finally be with my Mia again. I just wish I could have avenged her death as I wanted.

The night I found out that the Martelé were responsible, I went to Al Martelé's usual place of business, a sex club on the other side of the island.

Obviously he was expecting me. A Guerra cannot pass over their turf and not be noticed, especially not the Don of the Guerra. But my mind was elsewhere. I had no thought for the consequences of my actions. My only thoughts were to kill. An hour later I left, barely alive, having started the biggest war our organisation has ever seen.

"Marco, its time." Van places his hand on my shoulder and turns me around to face him. "Whatever happens, boss, it has been an honour to work alongside you."

Holding my hand out, I reply, "The pleasure was all mine, Van. Thank you—for everything. Now let's kill as many of these motherfuckers as we can and go out with a bang."

We leave the back garden and enter the house through the back door. The house now looks more like an armoury than a home. Each surface is covered in guns and ammunition. I wrap as many ammunition belts around me as I can, clip my communication radio to my belt, and pick up my machine gun.

"Boss, your vest."

Van throws me a bulletproof vest, but I let it drop to the floor. I have no intention of surviving today. A captain always goes down with his ship. After one last look at Van, who nods in acceptance, I make my way through the house to the front room where I will be stationed. We have ten men left in the Guerra. After months of bloodshed, too many men have lost their lives fighting for our name. Each remaining Guerra member is set up around the house, ready for battle.

The Martelé have outnumbered us. Over the past few years, they have been recruiting, waiting for their chance to take over. Unfortunately for us, that day has come. But they won't be getting past me that easily. Settled in the window with my gun pointing at the gate, I'm poised and ready for attack.

"Get ready," I instruct through the radio after seeing movement around the walls of the front gardens.

BOOM! There's a blast outside to my left. A large fireball shoots into the sky. Black smoke surrounds it.

BOOM! Another at the end of the driveway.

BOOM! A third blast to the surrounding walls on the right.

Once the fire turns into smoke, Martelé men appear, running towards the house, machine guns firing frantically in front of them. I shoot them one by one, not missing, each bullet reaching its destination, every man taking a hit. Bodies drop to their deaths on my front lawn. But they keep coming, one after another. It's like a conveyor belt of armed men.

I reload my gun over and over. Sweat pours from every part of my body, the sound of gunfire intensely vibrating my eardrums. I'm aware of explosions and shouting throughout the house, but I daren't take my focus off my job in hand for a second. After what feels like an eternity, Martelé men stop coming through the blown-out walls. When I stop shooting, everything is quiet. Too quiet.

"Marco Guerra." Al Martelé says my name sarcastically as he presses his gun into the back of my skull. The cold metal against my hot sweating head feels quite soothing.

"Al Martelé," I reply with the same sarcastic tone. "What took you so long."

"Stand," he orders. "Put your gun down."

I release my gun and place it on the windowsill. As I go to stand up, I feel the familiar sensation of a bullet piercing my skin and tendons. Falling forward, I catch myself on the window.

"I said stand the fuck up," Martelé orders again.

But I can't. My legs cannot hold my weight. I have been shot in both heels. My Achilles tendons are blown to smithereens. My inability to get up has the men behind me laughing. I quickly throw my upper body around, grab Al Martelé, and pull him to the floor. I wrap my hands around his neck and squeeze with every ounce of energy I have left. I'm beaten and shot again until I can no longer hold my grip. Al rolls around on the floor, coughing and gasping for air.

"Tie... him to a fucking... chair!" he orders, spluttering as he tries to catch his breath.

Martelé soldiers restrain me tightly and uncomfortably to a chair. I know I am in for a few long hours of torture. I made my peace with death a long time ago. Living a life like mine, you have to. Unfortunately my body has been trained to withstand hours of torture, which, when you want to die, isn't a good thing. It's not that I don't feel pain, but that I have trained my body not to react to it. Therefore, my blood pressure and heart rate will stay the same, and there will be no verbal or facial reaction. My breathing won't change, nor will the quickness of my reactions.

The next moment Van is brought into the room, not looking his best. He is tied to a chair next to me. I was hoping he had somehow managed to escape. No such luck, obviously.

"Ahh, wonderful. Now you are both here, we can start our meeting," Al says, still sounding hoarse from my strangulation. "I have some exciting news to tell you both. The Martelé have now taken over the whole of Itay." Al laughs.

Vans grunts. I keep quiet.

"We have now claimed the last of your territory, and once you die today, Marco Guerra, the Guerra bloodline will die with you. No more Guerras." He claps his hands in excitement.

This has been a worry for the Guerras for the last few generations. Each line has become smaller through death. Last in line before me was Leonardo Guerra, who needed to marry and have children, but as he and his wife died, that line ended there. I am only Leonardo's cousin, but still Guerra blood. I needed to have had children before I died for the line to continue.

"Van, I know the Alboni family have been very loyal to the Guerras through the generations. If you prove yourself, I may be able to find some work for a man like you." Al lights a cigarette as he speaks to Van.

"I'd rather die," Van spits.

"That can also be arranged," Al growls back. "Back to my exciting news. I have a new business partner." Al gestures towards the open door. "I think you already know Lorenzo."

Lorenzo enters with smuggest grin I have ever seen.

My body automatically lunges towards him in anger. Al and Lorenzo laugh as I fall face-first to the floor, still fastened to the chair. I'm left there for a few moments while they all have a good chuckle at my expense. The men continue to talk about their takeover plans. But I switch it off to focus on my own thoughts. I'm trying to pinpoint the exact time it all went wrong. Where I made my first mistake. What I could have done to change this outcome—when I hear a name that pulls me back to the present moment.

"Mia. Yes, that was all my idea," Lorenzo admits confidently.

My eyes bulge. "You bastard," I spit. Unfortunately, although my body has been trained to not respond to physical pain, I have no control over emotional pain. That must be what their plan is. Torture me with emotional pain that actually feels like physical pain.

"The plan did, however, take an unfortunate turn, but the results were what we wanted in the end," Al explains.

"Yes, that was unexpected," Lorenzo agrees.

Van pushes for more information on his sister. "What do you mean? Unexpected?"

"The plan was to kidnap Mia and hold her hostage in return for Marco surrendering enough territories over to the Martelé that the Martelé would be a majority leader. We had seen how much Mia had become to mean to Marco," Lorenzo explains.

My mind is goes crazy. So many questions. What happened? Why did she die?

"What changed, Martelé?" I demand.

"That is still a mystery." Martelé frowns and

rubs his chin. "We assumed you had worked out our plan and intercepted or Mia had fought back after her kidnapping, then in turn, the car lost control, and she blew them all up. It couldn't have gone any better for us, really. Mia dying meant we got more than we could have imagined."

"You're lying. Your men drove into Mia at speed and killed her. I've seen the CCTV!" Van shouts at them both.

"Enough!" Al Martelé demands. "I don't want to waste any more time here. You will both die now. You may have thought I'd draw your death out as long as I can, but you are already a pathetic broken man, Marco Guerra." Martelé then addresses the room. "Here, today, you will witness the death of the last Guerra. After this moment I do not want that name to ever be said again. The Guerra name dies with him."

I don't mind dying to save another person or for the future of my organisation. But to die like this, full of guilt and regret, is the worst death anyone could have. I drop my head in shame and wait.

Chapter 19

Mia

Thankfully I feel much better when I wake up. The first thing I see when I open my eyes is Donna's concerned face.

She smiles sweetly at me. "Arianna, you gave us quite a scare."

"I gave myself a scare," I admit, pushing my elbows into the bed and lifting myself into a more upright position. Donna helps by raising my bed. "What was that? Was it something to do with the accident or my brain?" I suddenly try and think of past memories before the accident, but no, it hasn't brought anything back.

"You had a severe allergic reaction and went into anaphylactic shock," Donna explains as she wraps a blood pressure cuff around my arm.

"What am I allergic to?"

"We are waiting for your test results to come back, but we are almost certain that you are severely allergic to peanuts."

"Wow. So is that something that has happened because of the accident?" I ask.

"It's very unlikely. Allergies, especially nut allergies, start in infanthood. I would assume this has been something you have had all your life, especially with how severe your reaction was. Your blood pressure is fine now." Donna removes the cuff from my arm.

"I don't understand. Eric said it was my favourite chocolate bar." This doesn't make any sense. "Argh! I'm so frustrated, Donna. I wish I could remember who I am."

Eric insists I wasn't allergic to nuts before my accident. The doctors have said it's very unusual, but not impossible. I don't believe him, though. I think he may be trying to kill me or the baby. Why, I'm not sure, but I will have to be careful once we are living together.

Over the next week, I work hard with the physios until I can walk well with crutches and get up and down stairs independently. I'm seventeen weeks pregnant now, and everything looks perfect with the baby. Once I have said goodbye to all the staff at the hospital and thanked them all for everything they done, Eric drives us to our home.

Along the way, we discuss living arrangements.

"I've made the bed up for you already. I've got you some new bedding. I hope you like it. I thought I would sleep in the spare room for now until you are fully recovered, but once the baby is born, I'll move in there with you, and the baby can have their own room."

"There's only two in the whole house? Only two bedrooms?" I demand in horror.

Eric laughs. "Yes, how many do you want?"

I will not be sharing a bed with this man. When I'm around him, I feel homesick.

After a journey of about twenty minutes, we pull down a narrow road only wide enough for one car. The road is bumpy, and the trees either side are so overgrown, their leaves scratch the car as we pass.

"Do we live down here?" I ask, staring out of the window.

"Yes, just a little further. There it is. All on its own. A lovely quiet spot with no neighbours to disturb us."

The house fills me with dread. I hadn't known what to expect, but I anticipated more than this tired little house. It's an old red brick house. The windows have wooden frames that are in desperate need of replacing. The roof sinks in on one side, and the front door looks multicoloured due to the many different coats of paint it's had over the years, which are now peeling off.

"It's a work-in-progress. We can do the house up together, make it our own. It's got lots of potential," Eric says proudly as he parks up next to the house.

I carefully get out of the car and walk up the overgrown path. It could be quite beautiful, actually. The gardens are surrounded by trees full of leaves blowing gently in the wind. My eyes are drawn to one tree in particular, a smaller tree at the side of the house. Being careful not to trip or get my crutches caught on the long grass, I make my way over to it. It's an apple tree. My arm naturally reaches up, and I pluck an apple from a low branch. I instantly bring it to my nose and breathe it in. The smell immediately brings a flash of a memory back. I'm doing the same thing—reaching for an apple, plucking it from a tree, and bringing it to my nose.

"Hey, Arianna, are you okay?" Eric comes jogging over, disturbing me from my moment.

"Yes, I'm fine. This is an apple tree."

"Oh yes, so it is. That will save us a bob or two on fruit, then." Eric laughs.

"Have I been here before?"

"Erm, no, you haven't. Come on, let's get you inside." Eric gently puts his hand on my elbow and ushers me towards the house.

I'm pleasantly surprised when we get inside. The place is clean and bright. It needs an update, but I think I might enjoy doing some interior designing. Eric shows me around. There's a decent size kitchen with a small table that would just about fit four people round it. The living room has two small sofas and a television on a cabinet. The bedrooms are both a similar size, with a double bed, bedside table, and wardrobe. There's only the one bathroom, which does bother me a little. The main thing I notice though is that everywhere is very bare. There are no photographs or belongings anywhere.

"Eric, where is all our stuff?"

"What stuff?" he asks evasively, knowing full well what I mean.

"Ornaments, photographs, paintings, anything?"

"Well, we are quite minimalistic, really, and the photographs I just haven't unpacked yet. Plus, if we are going to do some decorating, there's no point unpacking and packing again."

He does have a point. In my room, there are some clothes hanging in the wardrobe and some underwear in the drawer. Their style doesn't please me at all.

"Eric, I'm going to need some new clothes," I say, wide-eyed as I close my wardrobe door.

"Okay. When you're a bit stronger, I'll take you shopping," Eric agrees.

That evening we settle on the sofa to watch some television. The signal is rubbish. Eric spends ages messing about with the aerial, trying to get a clear picture.

"Argh, I will have to get on the roof tomorrow and sort it out. This will have to do for tonight—some foreign channel." Eric gives up and slumps on his sofa.

The *foreign* channel, as Eric put it, is showing a film with English subtitles. The film is Italian. The words have me smiling and relaxed. I get lost in the actors' voices. It gives me comfort, and I feel connected to it somehow.

"It's so strange, Eric. I understand every word they are saying. If anything, it feels more natural than English."

"Oh, really?" Eric replies, seeming uninterested.

"Yeah. Did I live in Italy when I was younger?" I ask as I watch the beautiful Italian scenery on the screen.

"No," he replies sharply.

"At the hospital, you said I didn't like to speak Italian. Why is that?" I'm sitting up straighter on the sofa now, feeling like this is something I need to know more about.

"Because it upset you. I don't know. Give it a rest, Arianna." Eric turns the television off.

"Hey, I was watching that!" I exclaim.

"I'm going to bed." Eric leaves in a huff.

What is his problem? I really think he doesn't want me to get my memory back. Well, if he isn't going to help me, I will do it on my own. I lift myself up off the sofa, hop across the room, and retrieve the remote control. I switch the television back on, and thankfully the film is still on. Lying down, I rub my tummy, feeling the little life growing inside me. With the Italian film and the sensation of little kicks and movements inside of me, for the first time since I woke up from my accident, I feel positive about my future.

After a couple of days of rest at home, Eric takes me into the village to do some shopping. It's a lovely little place, and everyone is so friendly. It seems like everyone knows each other and there's a strong community here. The village, albeit small, has everything you would need. There's a post office, butcher's, greengrocer—you name it, it's here. It even has a couple of boutique clothes shops, which are just what I need and a cosmetics store I am enjoying browsing in.

"Right, come on, Arianna, can we go now?"

Eric moans as he follows me around the makeup stands.

"Wait!" I exclaim as I'm filled with a sudden rush of familiarity.

"What is it?" Eric asks.

"MIA. This makeup brand. I recognise it." I pick up a lipstick and take off the lid, then twist it up to see the colour. The brightness of the red makes me smile. "Is this the brand I usually wear, Eric?"

"I don't know. I don't think you ever wore makeup," he replies, irritated.

I find his answer hard to believe given how strongly I am drawn to the red, glittering cosmetic stand.

"Is it okay if I just get a few bits?" I ask, hoping I haven't spent all Eric's money.

"Yes, just hurry up."

"Can I help you?" a very glamourous retail assistant asks.

"Yes please, that would be lovely. I need everything. A primer, foundation, concealer, the lot." The names of the types of products come out of my mouth like a reflex. "I had an accident a few months ago where I suffered burns to my face. They're healing well, but I'll need something that isn't going to affect the healing process."

"Absolutely no problem at all. We have some ultra-light products in the MIA sensitive range that will be perfect. You take a seat on the stool, and we will get to work selecting what is most suitable for your skin tone." The assistant helps me onto the stool and gets straight to work. "You know, I feel like I have met you before. What is your name?" she asks, while dabbing various products onto my face.

"Arianna. But I'm sorry, I wouldn't know if we had met before if we had. When I had my accident, I lost my memory. Do you think you might know me, then?"

"No, sorry I don't recognise the name. Maybe you just remind me of someone. Oh god, but how awful. I can't imagine how heartbreaking it must be to not remember who you are."

"Yeah, it's tough. But I have a feeling my memory will return any day now. I've already had a lot of familiar feelings." I say, which gets a quizzical look from Eric.

On the journey home, Eric is very quiet.

"Thanks for buying me everything today, Eric. I feel awful not having my own money. Once I've had the baby, I'll see about getting a job so I can help support us."

"There's no need. I earn enough for both of us," Eric replies.

"What is it you do? I know you work from home on your computer, but what are you actually doing?" I inquire.

"I'm an accountant for a large building company. It's easy enough. I can work where and when I want, and it pays well." He shrugs. "You just concentrate on our family."

Eric puts his hand on my stomach, and I have to fight the urge to push him away. It's his baby, too, so I have to let him share in it.

The next few months pass quickly. Eric and I have been renovating the house, and it looks pretty spectacular now. We have a new bathroom, which I tiled myself, a new kitchen that Eric and I fitted, and all the walls have been sanded and painted. We make a good team, surprisingly. Eric was kind enough to let me have free reign in the design. I have chosen all the décor, and I'm feeling more at home. I just wish I could shake this constant heartache. It's like I miss someone dreadfully, only I cannot remember who.

Now that the house is finished, I have been working on the garden. It's a nice sunny day today, so I leave Eric working on his computer and go outside. There are some waist-high planters I want to clear out, and with my bump getting quite large now, I need something to sit on to save my back. I remember seeing some old furniture in the shed when Eric was last in there, so I go and have a look at what I can find.

The shed is crammed full of junk. The gardening equipment is at the entrance along with the decorating tools we have used, but behind them are tables with boxes piled on top of each other. I carefully move things outside so I can get closer, hoping there's a chair or stool I can use.

When I get nearer to the boxes, I see they have writing on them. *Bedroom. Living room.* Curiosity takes over, and I begin opening the box marked *Bedroom.* Inside the items are wrapped in bubble wrap. I take out the first one and unravel it to find a photo frame with a wedding picture inside it. The date and "Arianna and Eric's wedding day" are written at the bottom. Eric looks quite handsome, smiling happily in his suit. The bride looks beautiful in a fitted white dress and veil. Only the bride… isn't me.

"What the hell are you doing in here!"

Erics voice makes me jump. So much so, the frame falls from my hands and smashes onto the floor.

Chapter 20

Marco

The rapid sharp bursts of machine guns fill my ears. Keeping my head down, I wait for my life to be taken. But when the sound quietens, and I realise I am still alive, I look up. The scene around me is surprising. Al Martelé lies lifeless on the floor. Lorenzo is slumped over him, the deep, crimson red of blood spreading across his white shirt. Martelé soldiers also cover the floor.

Confused, I look over at Van, who is still tied to his chair. He smirks as he watches me take in the room.

"How the fuck?" I ask, completely astounded by the situation around me.

Van looks at the door as if expecting someone. That's when I hear the heavy footsteps in the hall. A suited man surrounded by smoke arrives in the doorway. He takes a drag of a cigar and blows it towards me.

"Leo Guerra," I choke as the smoke clears, and his smug-looking face becomes visible.

"What took you so long?" Van laughs.

What the fuck is going on here? I stare at them both in disbelief, and they roar with laugher.

"Aren't you supposed to be fucking dead?" I boom.

"Had to come and save your sorry ass, didn't I," Leo says as he unties Van from the chair.

"What have you fucking done! You died so you and your wife could live. Now you have just put another bounty on both your heads!" I'm furious. Why would he come back and risk everything we fought so hard to protect?

Leo moves to stand in front of me. His face is stern as he looks fiercely into mine. "Marco. My sole purpose has always been to protect my family. You are my family. I wouldn't even be alive now if it wasn't for the many times you have saved my life. Now don't ever question my judgement again."

Leo uses his knife to release me from my restraints. I stand up immediately but fall into Leo's arms.

"Shit, look at the state of you." Leo sits me back in the chair and assesses my heels. "Van, contact our medics at the hospital. Tell them Marco needs emergency surgery and that it is even more imperative that our presence is keep confidential."

"On it."

Van and Leo carry me into the car. At this point my adrenaline has worn off, and the pain is excruciating. My lack of blood has me dozing in and out of consciousness. I'm relieved when we arrive at the hospital and I'm sedated. The pain in my body and heart finally numb, I'm grateful to be at peace from my own deafening thoughts.

When I begin to come round after my operation, I hear Van and Leo talking in the room beside me.

"What's the plan, then, boss? Surely we can expect a retaliation from the Martelé?" Van asks Leo.

"It won't be for a while. The next bloodline leader of the Martelé is Al Martelé's son. But he is only twelve years old. Therefore, the leadership will go to a cousin. There are five cousins who will need to prove themselves as capable. Fortunately, this gives us some time," Leo explains. "In the meantime, we need to build ourselves back up. Bigger and stronger than ever."

In my state of slumber, my mind goes to Mia. My anger builds as I remember Lorenzo's involvement. But there's something that isn't feeling right. Lorenzo said they had only planned to kidnap Mia. I didn't believe him at that moment, but why would he lie? He had no reason to. He was happy to take the credit of the original idea being his own, so why not her death?

I sit bolt upright in bed. Alarms sound as I rip monitors from my chest in the process.

"Hey, relax. You're in hospital. Your surgery is done, the bullets have been removed, and your tendons are now reattached. Bloody magicians, these doctors," Leo explains, putting his hand on my shoulder.

A nurse comes to my aid, reconnecting the monitors and turning off the alarms.

"No, I need to get up. I need to see that CCTV footage again."

"No, you need to rest, and that is an order," Leo demands. "If you don't rest, you will ruin any chance you have of walking again, and I need you to help sort out this fucking mess."

"Van. What Lorenzo said. There is more to it. Something else happened that night. I need to find out what," I plead to Van.

He nods in a reluctant acceptance. I know watching that video was hard for Van, and I'm sure he never wants to watch it again. But he understands how much guilt I feel.

"Tell me everything from the beginning." Leo sits back in a chair at my side, while Van and I go over the painful events. Leo assures me we will find out the truth. They leave me to rest while they go and make some calls.

The next day, Leo and Van bring a laptop into the hospital.

"We have the CCTV. I got the IT team to clean it up. It's much clearer now." Leo sets the laptop down on my bed without making eye contact. His expression is blank, which means he is hiding his true feelings.

"There's something on here, isn't there?"

"Just watch," Van says as he wakes up the screen and presses play.

The pain I first felt when watching the final moments of my Mia's life return. I watch as the girls quickly leave the bar, their guards chasing after them. Why were they running from the guards? They're arguing with them outside, so much so, they don't notice the car speeding along the road and heading towards them. The car mounts the pavement, and Mia penetrates the windscreen.

But the car doesn't stop. It continues at speed before it crashes into a similar oncoming car. They collide headfirst at speed. The first car mounts the second, flips backwards, and lands on its roof. Seconds later the car explodes into flames, and the video ends. I have so many questions, but I didn't see anything new.

I look at Leo and Van.

"It's okay. She's my sister and I didn't notice either," Van says as he rewinds the video and pauses the picture on Mia and her friends outside the bar.

Leo points at Mia. "That is not Mia." He then brings up an image of the girls when they entered the bar. They are wearing the same outfits, but there is something different about them. "Mia is taller than Marisa and Lucia." He then flips back to the image just before the accident and points at Mia again. Mia is noticeably shorter.

"What the...." My mind whirls with the information. What does this mean? Where is Mia?

After going back to the CCTV of the inside of the bar, Leo rewinds thirty minutes before the accident. We watch as Mia, Marisa, and Lucia enter the ladies' bathroom. A moment later three other women also enter. After a while, Mia exits on her own, then circulates the room before returning to the bathroom.

"What is she up to?" I wonder out loud.

After another twenty-five minutes, the three girls exit the bathroom.

"They switched clothes," I say in disbelief.

"After watching this video, I checked the surveillance at the side of the building." Leo then brings up another screen with the image of an alleyway.

It's dark and very grainy. At first the screen is still, but then movement to the side catches my eye. I can just about make out the outline of three women. The closer they get to the camera, the clearer they become. Marisa, Lucia, and my Mia. The three women continue down the alley away from the bar and dump something in a bin before disappearing from sight.

"That wasn't Mia we saw getting hit by the car," Van explains.

"Then where the fuck is she?" Could it be true? Is my Mia still alive? But if she were, why hasn't she come home or contacted someone? The last location on her phone was in that area. Why didn't she take her phone with her?

"I just don't understand what she was doing. Did she know the Martelé were after her? Was this her plan to escape?" Van runs his hands over his face in frustration.

"No," I disagree. "Mia would never purposely put another person's life in danger, even to save her own. She used them as a distraction to get away from the guards. It wouldn't surprise me if those friends of hers had something to do with it either. They probably wanted a night out in London, free to do as they please."

"Only they didn't get their night out. Something happened to them when they left the bar. I have my contacts in the UK gathering all the

CCTV footage in that area," Leo explains.

"We did all that. We were there after the accident," Van states

"Yes, but we are looking for something different now. We are looking for the girls alive, wearing different clothes. I've also asked for the police reports for all surrounding areas on that night. We will find out what happened to Mia."

My heart and my head are playing against each other. My heart says Mia is alive and that I knew it all along, while my head is sure Mia is dead. Okay, she didn't die the way we originally thought, but there is no way that Mia would not contact me or her family if she was.

"I need to go to London. How am I fixed for traveling?" I ask.

Leo dismisses me. "You are not fixed at all."

"Get me some crutches. I'll manage."

Leo dismisses me again. "No fucking way."

"If you don't help me, I will do it on my own. I need to go to London," I insist, deadly serious.

Leo groans in annoyance. "You're a fucking pain in my arse!"

Chapter 21

Mia

"Ahh, shit." Some of the glass from the frame has cut the top of my foot. I knew sliders weren't the best choice of footwear for gardening. "Bloody hell, Eric. You've got some explaining to do," I say, picking out the glass from my foot.

I retrieve the wedding photo from the floor. Eric looks at me quizzically. He's probably surprised I haven't attempted to kill him yet. The thing is, I'm not at all surprised it isn't me in this picture.

"Help me out of here. I'm going to need to do something with this cut. It's pretty deep."

Eric takes my hand and assists me out of the cramped shed. Once inside the house, I use the first aid kit to clean up my wound and use steri-strips to close the cut. Eric hasn't said a word since coming in from the shed, other than to comply when I've asked for something regarding my injury. But now he is going talk.

"Who am I, Eric?"

"You're Arianna."

His reply makes me angry. "Stop fucking lying, Eric. This is Arianna." I throw their wedding photograph at him. "And that is clearly not me."

Eric picks up the photo and sighs. He lightly rubs his thumb over the image of Arianna.

"Who am I, Eric?" I ask again.

"I don't know."

I was afraid that might be his answer. I think I've known from first waking up in the hospital that I wasn't Arianna. But with no memory, it's very difficult to trust your instincts. There must be a link between myself and Arianna for this situation to be possible.

"Where is the real Arianna?" I ask, frustrated.

"I don't know." Eric puts his head in his hands.

"There's a lot of don't knows here, Eric. Tell me something you do know. Tell me why you have been pretending I am Arianna."

Eric just shakes his head. His face is still in his hands, and he's slumped over in the chair he is sat in.

"Start from the beginning. You find out I'm in hospital. Who rang you? What did they say?" I ask, trying to sound calm.

I need him to explain everything to me so I have the best chance of finding out who I am. Inside, however, I am raging. I've been told the story of my accident many times. Eric has told me, and Donna my nurse at the hospital discussed it with me, trying to jog my memory. But nothing ever came back. The only thing I think may be related is a reoccurring dream where I'm running to something or someone, but I don't get there in time, and then harrowing screams follow. According to what I've been told, I went out one evening with my two friends, we exited a bar, and were talking to the bouncers when a car came at speed, mounted the pavement, and drove straight into us. The car then collided with an oncoming car, which caused the car to explode, hence the burns.

"Arianna left me a couple of months before the accident. I'd apologised over and over and begged her to come back, but she wouldn't. She'd just got this new job, and her work friends turned her against me. I knew I shouldn't have let her get a job, but she'd kept going on and on about wanting to earn her own money. So I'd given in." Eric shakes his head angrily. "But then I get a call from the hospital saying my wife had been in an accident. Since we're still married, I'm her next of kin. Finally Arianna had come back to me." Eric smiles.

"But she hadn't—it was me. So why didn't

you tell the hospital I wasn't Arianna when you got there?" I can't believe something like this could happen.

"At first I thought you were Arianna. Your face was covered with bandages, your hair is the same colour, and you were found with Arianna's bag and identification. I went to the hospital every day and sat by your side, praying for you to get better and for another chance to be with you."

"When did you realise it wasn't Arianna lying in that bed?" I cannot comprehend why someone could lie about a person's life.

"When they removed the bandages from your face. I was so shocked, I left the hospital without speaking to anyone. I didn't go back for days. I was heartbroken you weren't Arianna, which meant the real Arianna must have died in the accident. But then I started to think about you. You only had me. When I got back to the hospital, you woke up. The doctors and nurses naturally told you your name was Arianna. When you said you couldn't remember who you were, I realised it must be God who had sent you to me. He was giving me a second chance to be a good husband. And then when I found out you were pregnant, I knew you were both a gift from him. Arianna and I had tried for years to have a child, but it had sadly never happened."

Eric looks at me hopefully. He actually

believes this bullshit about me being a gift from God. He has given me some good information to go on, though. I was obviously with Arianna that night. Eric said she was out with work friends, so it's possible I worked with Arianna. I'll find out where that was and go see if anyone knows who I am.

"You said I—well, Arianna—didn't work when I asked you. Why was that?"

"I didn't want you contacting them. They would know that you weren't Arianna," Eric admits.

"Okay, tell me where she used to work. Maybe I worked there too. Someone might know my real identity." I take a piece of paper and a pen out of the kitchen drawer, ready to write down the name of the company.

"No!" Eric snatches the pen out of my hand. "You can't leave me. I won't let you."

"Eric, you must realise I'm not actually a gift from God. I have a life. I might even have a husband. This baby obviously isn't yours. Someone somewhere is missing me."

"Well, nobody has come looking for you, have they?"

"Probably because they think I am dead!" I exclaim. Oh god, my family will think I am dead. It's been over six months since my accident now.

Their lives will have moved on. "Tell me where she worked!"

I'm angry now. But by the look on Eric's face, so is he. Eric raises his hand to strike me across the face, but my reactions are faster. Forcefully grabbing hold of his wrist, I knee him in the groin. As he bends over in pain, I twist his arm around his back, pulling it painfully from its socket.

"Huh, I didn't know I could do that." I nod, proud of myself. It seems muscle memory is a lot stronger than brain memory.

As I'm deciding what my next move will be, I feel a mild popping sensation down below, which is followed by a gush of fluid that pours down my legs.

"Oh shit." I release Eric and hold my stomach. "No, no little baby, you're not due for another month or so yet." Forgetting everything else and focusing on my baby, I tell Eric, "I'm going to clean myself up and get changed, and then you can drive me to the hospital. Get the hospital bags ready. I'll only be a minute."

I grab a change of clothes and have a quick shower. Once I'm dressed, I go to look for Eric. I find him sat at the kitchen table with a large knife in front of him.

"What are you doing, Eric? We need to go." I have a bad feeling about this. Protecting my baby is my uttermost priority.

"I'm not taking you to the hospital."

"I'll get a taxi, then."

As I walk over to the house phone, I notice the extra bolts on the door have been padlocked so they can't be opened. Looks like I'm going to have a fight on my hands.

"You're not going anywhere, Arianna. You can have the baby here, in our home."

"The baby is early. It might need some medical care. I'm not having it here. Neither of us knows what we doing—it's too dangerous. Come on, Eric, please—where's the keys to locks?"

I feel remarkably calm, considering the situation I am in. My only concern is my baby and that knife. Eric doesn't reply. The locks don't actually bother me. There are plenty of windows in this house I can easily break and get out of. I just don't want to turn my back on Eric while he is in this state.

"I'm telling you now, Eric—I am leaving this house and going to the hospital. I will either go through the door or the window. You will not stop me." I'm ready to fight for my baby.

Eric stands up and picks up the knife.

"I can't let you leave me again, Arianna. I can't live without you."

"I'm not Arianna. I'm...."

My name is on the tip of my tongue. I'm feeling more and more myself. I'm a strong capable woman. Looking at the knife Eric is pointing towards me, I know what I have to do. I act fast so he has no time to respond. My reflexes are precise and forceful. While holding his arm at his back, I release the knife from his hand. Then I wrap my arm around his neck. I put my left hand on the back of his head and tilt it forward to keep control of him. He's trying his best to fight back, but I'm much stronger and faster than him.

Suddenly I get a flashback, like a reel of memories lasting seconds. I'm doing self-defence with a trainer. Then I'm fighting for my life against a large man wearing black. All these snippets of memories have a soundtrack of harrowing female screams. I know those voices.

I apply pressure to the sides of Eric's neck by squeezing my arm, cutting off the blood supply to his brain. Once his body goes limp, I sit him down on a chair. I find the duct tape and secure his arms behind him, a leg to each chair leg, and then use the rest to wrap his body against the back of the chair. There's no chance he is coming after me. After sticking a little piece over his mouth for added discomfort, I find the keys to the padlocks in Eric's pocket, along with the car keys.

Once I'm out of the house, I get into Eric's car. I hope I can drive. After turning on the engine, I put my foot on the clutch and put the car into reverse. I *do* know how to drive. As I set off down the narrow lane that leads to our house, a flashback of a red Ferrari makes me smile. A little kick from my baby has me rubbing my bump. "Everything is going to be just fine, I promise."

"Arggh!" My first contraction makes me slam on the break. "Breathe, Mia. Breathe."

Oh my god. My name is Mia.

Again I'm hit with a flashback reel. It's of different people, all saying my name. "Mia." "Mia." "Mia."

Once the pain subsides, I continue my journey to the hospital. I'm not one hundred percent sure where the hospital is, but I know it isn't far. I'll just ask someone for directions when I get to the main road. A minute later I'm hit with another contraction, and they don't stop there. They're coming thick and fast now, and I have to keep stopping the car to breathe through them. I've been driving along the main road for what seems like hours, and I haven't seen one person or even a car to stop and ask for directions.

"Finally," I say to my rearview mirror as I see a car pull into the lay-by I'm resting in.

Chapter 22

Marco

On the jet over to England, Leo goes through the police reports he's been sent from his contacts in the UK.

"Damien said it's a mess. The police didn't follow up in so many areas. For example, this."

Leo passes me a folder. I open it and read the first page, which is an evidence sheet. The crime scene is detailed. *Two women in their thirties found dead in Beacons Alley. Both women had gunshot wounds that were determined as their cause of death.*

"Look at the photos at the back," Leo suggests.

I take out the images from the back of the folder and instantly recognise them as Marisa and Lucia.

"They were found meters away from where the accident happened, yet the police thought they were unrelated," Leo explains.

All I can do is shake my head. Leo then

passes me another folder.

"These are the DNA results from the wreckage and Mia."

The police took DNA from both Van and their father to run a DNA match for Mia. Her body had been so badly crushed and burnt in the accident, they couldn't positively identify her from her dental records. The results showed a match of DNA to theirs in what was left of the car. But the DNA on Mia's body showed *inconclusive.*

"Inconclusive. What does that mean?" I ask.

"It means my fucking father didn't read it properly. It means the DNA of the body wasn't a match, it should have been tested again. But it wasn't." Van is furious.

"And there's more." Leo passes me and Van another file. Van obviously isn't aware of the information in this file.

"There were six bodies pulled from the wreckage. Two dead guards. Three dead females, and one alive female. Name: Arianna Wake." Leo gestures for us to open the file.

Inside are Arianna's medical notes. It lists the extensive injuries she received from the accident. Burns, fractures, head injury. But watch catches my eye are the words *memory loss.*

I'd found it hard to believe that Mia could still be alive and not have contacted anyone she knew. But if she had lost her memory, that would explain everything.

When I look up from the folder, Leo and Van are staring at me. But both look incredibly blurry. That's when I notice the tears in my eyes as they fall down my face.

"She's alive?" I ask, hoping this isn't a dream.

"It looks that way," says Leo with a little smile.

We sit in silence for the rest of the flight. My thoughts are completely with Mia. I'm worried for her safety. The medical notes said her next of kin was her husband and that she had been discharged form hospital to return home with him. If he has laid a finger on her, I will kill him. I feel sick at the thought of another man near her. But it has been over six months now since the accident. She obviously still doesn't remember who she is or who I am. What if she now loves this man who is her assumed husband?

"What I don't understand is why this guy is saying he's her husband when he's clearly not," says Van in car from the airport. "And where is his actual wife?"

"His wife is probably one of the dead women. He's obviously a psychopath," I state angrily, infuriated that this man is with my Mia. "How long till we get there?"

"Another five minutes. You're going to have to be patient, Marco. Mia may still not have regained her memory, and we don't want to scare her. The police are meeting us there, and once we confirm it is Mia, they will arrest Eric Wake. I've also asked for a medical team to check her over while we are there."

Leo's words sadden me.

I've dreamed so many times of somehow finding Mia alive. Although we are about to see Mia in the flesh, it might not be Mia in her mind.

When we arrive at the house, I get out of the car alone. I've insisted I go in first alone for many reasons, like not having any witnesses if I kill the man. But mostly because I want the first person Mia sees to be me. Using my crutches, I hop up the path of a well-kept front garden and knock on the door.

Chapter 23

Mia

The driver gets out of the car behind me, and I'm glad to see it is a woman. I thought for second Eric may have gotten loose and come after me. I should have known better, there's no way he can get out of my restraints by himself. When I get out of the car to join her, I'm struck with another contraction. This one is so intense, my knees buckle, and I have to lean on the car to hold myself up.

The elderly woman states the obvious. "Oh dear, are you in labour? You need to get to the hospital."

"Yes, can you tell me the way?" I ask through breathing exercises.

"I can do better than that. I'll take you. But we will have to use your car. I've got a flat tire."

"That's fine. Please just get me there." I think I'm starting to get the urge to push. This baby is going to be here very soon.

"You get in the car. I just need to get Mr.

Pickles." The lady opens her passenger door and retrieves a small pug.

I love dogs. The images of dogs flash through my mind, making me smile.

It's only a short ride to the hospital from here, thank goodness.

After thanking the lady for her generosity, I'm wheeled into the maternity unit by a nurse who was thankfully at the door when I arrived.

"It looks like you got here just in time," the midwife informs me during my examination. "Now, baby is a little early, so we have got everything ready just in case they need a little help. But don't worry, at thirty-six weeks, babies are pretty much cooked." She laughs at her own joke.

A noise sounds on the monitor I'm now attached to just as another contraction begins.

"Looks like you're ready to push. Come on, Arianna, you can do this."

I listen to my body and push when I feel the urge. I take in everything the midwife says and focus completely on bringing my baby safely into the world. The more I focus on my child, the more of myself comes back to me. When I think of taking my child home, I see my house. My old Italian farmhouse. My home, the home I renovated myself. With each push, I receive more of myself, of my life, my real life.

"Just one more, Arianna. You are doing fantastically," says my midwife encouragingly.

Finding the last of my strength, I give birth to my child.

"It's a girl. Congratulations, Mummy, you have a beautiful daughter."

The midwife places my baby on my chest. Our eyes lock, and she gives me the last bit of myself. "Marco."

I cry with happiness into my daughter. She is the image of him. His eyes, his nose. She's beautiful. I can't believe we created this amazing human. My heart aches for Marco. He must think I am dead or I am sure he would have come for me. As I stare into the eyes of my daughter, I'm filled with gratitude. After all the months of not knowing who I am, *she found me.* Marco is going to have the shock of his life. This whole situation is mind blowing. I know there are going to be hard times ahead. But with my daughter in my world, I can face anything. My name is Mia Alboni, and I am a woman of the Guerra Mafia.

"She is beautiful, just like her mummy," the midwife coos at my side.

"Oh, that's all her father. She is just like him." I smile.

"Have you thought of any name yet?" she

asks.

"I haven't decided. I'd like to speak to her father before I make that decision."

"Oh, good—I thought that when you said *Marco* when she was born, you were naming her that. Marco's a nice name for a boy, but not a pretty girl like her," the midwife admits.

"Don't worry, that's not her name. It's' her father's name. Her father is Marco Guerra."

As the words leave my mouth, the door to the room opens with a creak. My heart floods with emotion when I see who stands in the doorway.

Chapter 24

Marco

The force of my knocking has opened the door to the house. It mustn't have been closed properly. Pushing it open with my crutch, I enter. Although I know I have never been in this house before, it somehow feels familiar. The first door I get to is the bathroom. A bathroom I have seen before. It is almost an exact replica for Mia's bathroom. The tiles on the walls are the same, the flooring exactly the same. The bath and shower are so similar, I swear I'm at her house in Italy. Continuing through the house, I enter the living room. Again this room has a very Mia feel to it. The colours and soft furnishings are just as Mia has at home.

When I make my way into the kitchen, I see a man restrained to a chair, duct tape around each leg, fastening them to the chair's. The tape around his hands and body holds him tight, preventing any movement. A small piece covers his mouth. I smile to myself; If the house furnishings weren't a positive confirmation that this is where Mia has been living, the situation of the man in front of me certainly proves she was here. I taught her well.

Taking in the pathetic man in front of me, I can't help but feel immense anger for him keeping my Mia away from me. I have no idea how he has treated her since she has known him, but it's obvious from the way he is restrained today that he hasn't been the perfect gentleman.

I rip the tape from his mouth, hoping it stings like hell.

"Eric Wake, I presume." I stand in front of him as he takes in my size.

His eyes are wide, and his body shakes in fear. "Who are you?" he asks.

"I am your worst fucking nightmare," I reply, meaning every word. "Where is Mia?"

"I don't know who you mean," he lies.

I thrust my crutch into his chest with so much force, his chair falls backwards and his head hits the floor. He cries out in pain at the impact. Then I return him to a sitting position by pulling the chair leg towards me.

"I will ask you again. The woman who has been living here with you—where is she?" I demand, hoping he answers, otherwise I don't think I can restrain myself from torturing him for the information I need. I don't think that would go down too well with the police who are waiting outside.

"She's gone to the hospital. General Hospital, I would think," Eric says, seeming genuine.

Although I want to inflict pain on this man who has had a hand in keeping me away from my Mia, I don't have time. I need to get to the hospital. We leave Eric with the police and head straight there.

"Did he say why she had gone to the hospital?" Van enquires when he pulls the car into the hospital car park.

"No. I'll just go to the main entrance and give her name. You both wait here. Once I've found her, I will call you to come in."

At the desk I give her name. "Mia…. Actually, try Arianna Wake."

"Ahh, yes. Straight down to the bottom of the corridor, turn left through the double doors, and then she will be in the first door on the left."

"Thanks," I say, hoping I can remember all those directions.

The closer I get to her room, the slower my pace gets. What do I say to her? What if she doesn't recognise me? Do I tell her who I am? I should have discussed this with Leo and Van. But I push my worries aside, knowing that the most important thing is that she is safe and well. Everything else, we can sort out in time. Placing my hand on the doorhandle, I take a deep breath. As I lean against the door to open it, I hear my Mia's voice. A sound that fills me with life. It's like my heart begins to beat fully again.

Her next words have my head spinning.

"That's her father's name. Her father is Marco Guerra."

When my eyes land on Mia, she is an absolute vision. Her cheeks are flushed, and her eyes sparkle. On her chest lies a small head covered in dark hair. Mia has a baby. My baby?

We stare at each other for a moment, neither of us believing what we are seeing.

The midwife releases us from our trance. "Come in, come in. I'll give you two some space." She ushers me in and leaves, closing the door behind her.

Mia holds out her hand. "Marco, come meet your daughter."

I throw down my crutches and take it in mine, kissing the back of her fingers. My other hand goes to the head of my daughter. That's something I never thought I would say.

"I can't believe this, Mia. I am so sorry. I thought you were dead. If I had known you were still alive, I would have come for you straight away." I bow my head in shame.

"You are here now. That's all that matters."

Mia wraps her arm around my neck.

When I look up, both Mia's and our daughter's eyes are on me. They both gaze at me with love. The power of that emotion gives me all the strength I need. I. Marco Guerra, will forever protect my girls. I will fight for them and my organisation to ensure their safety. And in that moment, they give me the greatest gift. They give me my life back.

Mia

I am overwhelmed with emotion. After Marco rings Van to let him know I am okay, the midwife returns and helps Marco get comfortable in a chair so he can hold our daughter.

"She seems absolutely fine, considering she is a little early, but the doctor will be along soon to check her over," the midwife says as she places our child in Marco's arms.

She looks even smaller now in the arms of her father. His body is stiff and awkward as he holds her. He's obviously worried about hurting her. His face, however, is the softest I have ever seen it. I enjoy watching them, and I take a mental picture, knowing I will never take my memories for granted again. Marco begins to relax as he gets used to the feeling of holding a baby. I notice the support braces around both of his legs and wonder what trouble he has got himself into while we have been apart. We have so much to catch up on. I have so much to catch up on with everyone. My thoughts turn to Marisa and Lucia. A sharp twist in my stomach has me gasping out. Marco looks at me with concern.

"Are you okay? Nurse!" he shouts, panicked, not being able to get up to come to me.

"I'm okay. I just remembered what happened to Marisa and Lucia. It's all been coming back to me a bit at a time since I started labour."

"I'm so sorry I wasn't there, Mia." Marco has a mixture of anger and guilt in his expression.

I just shake my head unable to respond. None of this was his fault.

While the midwife checks me over Van's large frame enters my room. I have never been so pleased to see my big brother. The smile on his face as he sees me has my eyes filling with tears. Van is a man who, again, like all Guerra men, never shows his feelings. So when he comes and gives me a hug, I know that whatever has happened and whatever the future shall bring, my daughter and I will have the best men by our sides.

After a week in hospital, having had every test available at the request of an overprotective Marco, we are both discharged and told we are fit to fly home to Italy. I need no further treatment for my burns. My skin is healing nicely, the neurology scans have shown a full recovery in my brain, and my memory has completely returned. Our little bundle of joy is strong and feeding well. It's funny, I feel like she has always been in my life.

"I think I have decided on a name, if it's all right with you," I say to Marco in the car on the way to the airport.

"I told you the decision is yours, Mia. Whatever you are happy with, so am I."

"What do you think about Larisa?" I ask hopefully.

"I think it is perfect," he says, giving me a little squeeze, understanding the merging of my friends' names.

When we arrive home, it feels very surreal. I realise now that when I was choosing all the décor for Eric's house, I was recreating my own in Italy without even realising it.

"See, Larisa? Have a look around. This is your home."

I beam with pride as catch my reflection in the mirror, holding our baby. Me, a mum. It's something I never thought I wanted, but I'm so incredibly grateful to be one now. Marco follows behind us as I go through the house and outside. I can't wait to see all my animals in the sanctuary.

"Mia! You're home." Emmaline runs towards me and embraces me in a hug, being careful not to squash Larisa. Emmaline cries with joy. "I can't believe what you have been through, I can't believe that psycho of a man got away with such a lie and nobody at the hospital realised." It is amazing really, and if it wasn't for the fact I can imitate the English accent perfectly, he probably wouldn't have got away with it.

Emmaline wipes the tears from her eyes. "I'm so sorry. But look at this beautiful girl," she gushes stroking Larisa's cheek.

"I'm fine, Emmaline, really. Marco tells me you have been taking care of the sanctuary while I have been gone. I really appreciate it. Thank you."

"Don't mention it. Now come on, all the animals are dying to see you."

When we get to the door, I hand Larisa over to Marco so I can greet the animals. As soon as we open the door, I am swarmed with wagging tails and kisses. After saying hello to my old friends along with some new ones, I notice my little pal is missing.

"Tipsy?" I ask Emmaline, concerned.

Emmaline looks from me to Marco with a smile on her face.

"Tipsy lives with me now. She's currently with the housekeeper. I'll bring her back later,"

Marco admits sheepishly while gently rocking our daughter.

Marco

The minute we return to Italy, my work in rebuilding the Guerra empire begins. It's going to take a lot of hard work, but with my woman by my side, I know anything is possible. The plus side to being with an independent, powerful woman like Mia is that she also lives and breathes the Guerra. Together we will come out on top and even stronger. Leo has returned to the dead, and although he got away without anyone knowing of his resurrection, I don't think that will be the last I see of him.

Today is the day of Larisa's christening. The ceremony is taking place in the grounds of Mia's home. Our home. I decided to move in with Mia when we returned. I couldn't face going back to my house, the place where I had broken. The place where I thought Mia had been buried. Arianna's ashes have now been returned to England where they belong, and the house and garden are now used for work purposes. Mia hadn't objected to my insistence on being a *roommate*, so here we are, a family of three.

It's a beautiful day, and Mia has done an incredible job organising a beautiful setup for our daughter. Only, it isn't just for Larisa, it is for Mia too. Today Mia and I will be getting married. She has no idea. We aren't even engaged. I know she has been hoping for a proposal, but I just thought we would get married instead.

When it is time for the ceremony, our family and friends take their seats, and Mia, holding Larisa, and I stand at the altar. Mia looks beautiful in a white dress that matches our very smiley, happy daughter. I wrap my arm around Mia as we stand and face the priest.

"Dearly beloved, we are gathered here today in the sight of God and in the presence of family and friends to join together Marco and Mia in holy matrimony."

Mia's face is a picture. Her mouth is agape, and her eyes sparkle with tears threatening to overspill.

"Is this okay?" I ask hopefully.

Mia nods. "Perfect." She beams.

Taking Larisa from Mia, I pass her to Emmaline, who is waiting behind us. She then passes a bouquet of flowers to Mia.

The priest continues. "As Marco and Mia have consented together in holy wedlock, and have witnessed the same before God and this company, and there to have given and pledged their faith each to the other, and have declared the same by giving and receiving a ring, and by joining hands, I pronounce that they are husband and wife, in the name of the Father, and of the Son, and of the Holy Spirit. Amen. You may now kiss your bride."

So, I do, over and over, for the rest of my life.

The End. Thank you for reading I hope you enjoyed Mia and Marcos story.

Next in the Found series we have more from Leo and Katie, coming later this year.

Acknowledgement

To my wonderful parents.

Thank you for your love and encouragement and for helping me believe I can achieve anything in the world.

I am so grateful you are mine.

About The Author

Joy Mullett

Joy Mullett has turned her obsession with reading into writing. Being a lover of romance with a big imagination Joy writes exciting and thrilling stories which are impossible to put down.

Follow Joy on Instagram, Tiktok and Facebook for her lastest updates and releases.

Printed in Great Britain
by Amazon